THE SQUAD

BLACK OP

Tom Palmer is an author and football fan. He is a frequent visitor to schools and libraries to talk about reading, writing and football. He has also worked with the National Literacy Trust, the Reading Agency and the Premier League Reading Stars scheme in his quest to promote a passion for reading among boys.

Tom is the author of the Football Academy and Foul Play series. He lives in Yorkshire with his family where he loves to watch football and run.

Find out more about Tom and read his blog at *www.tompalmer.co.uk*

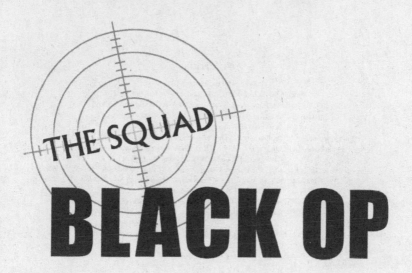

THE SQUAD

BLACK OP

TOM PALMER

PUFFIN

PUFFIN BOOKS

Published by the Penguin Group
Penguin Books Ltd, 80 Strand, London WC2R ORL, England
Penguin Group (USA) Inc., 375 Hudson Street, New York, New York 10014, USA
Penguin Group (Canada), 90 Eglinton Avenue East, Suite 700, Toronto, Ontario, Canada M4P 2Y3
(a division of Pearson Penguin Canada Inc.)
Penguin Ireland, 25 St Stephen's Green, Dublin 2, Ireland (a division of Penguin Books Ltd)
Penguin Group (Australia), 250 Camberwell Road, Camberwell, Victoria 3124, Australia
(a division of Pearson Australia Group Pty Ltd)
Penguin Books India Pvt Ltd, 11 Community Centre, Panchsheel Park, New Delhi – 110 017, India
Penguin Group (NZ), 67 Apollo Drive, Rosedale, Auckland 0632, New Zealand
(a division of Pearson New Zealand Ltd)
Penguin Books (South Africa) (Pty) Ltd, Block D, Rosebank Office Park, 181 Jan Smuts Avenue,
Parktown North, Gauteng 2193, South Africa

Penguin Books Ltd, Registered Offices: 80 Strand, London WC2R ORL, England

puffinbooks.com

First published 2012
005

Text copyright © Tom Palmer, 2012
All rights reserved

The moral right of the author has been asserted

Set in 13/16pt Baskerville MT Std
by Palimpsest Book Production Limited, Falkirk, Stirlingshire
Printed in Great Britain by Clays Ltd, St Ives plc

British Library Cataloguing in Publication Data
A CIP catalogue record for this book is available from the British Library

ISBN: 978-0-141-33778-4

www.greenpenguin.co.uk

To Nikki Woodman.
Lovely neighbour. Lovely friend.
Lovely woman.

DEATH IN THE DESERT

Three small figures moved rapidly across the night-time desert floor, sliding over shifting sands, keeping low.

Low because if they were visible they could be shot within seconds.

They stopped when they located a flickering light coming from an isolated camp. Their target. They knew from satellite images taken earlier in the day that the camp consisted of a large tent, a fire, a dozen camels, a Land Rover and a small army of men. They also knew that the target was heavily armed and, no doubt, under strict orders to fire at anything that moved. It was the base of one of the most dangerous terrorist cells in the world and it would be well defended.

The three figures had to get close to the tent without being spotted and listen to what was being planned.

It was a tough mission, but the trio was up to the job.

*

Rob, Lesh and Lily worked for the British government, half of a team of six who were deployed around the world and were known as the Squad. They were extremely clever, highly trained and had already been involved in a number of successful missions. The only difference between them and the other spies working for the British government was that they were all just thirteen years old.

Each of them had a role or a speciality that made them perfect for this mission.

Rob – tall, with short black hair – was the leader. His job: to make decisions and give orders.

Lezsek – or Lesh as he liked to be known – was in charge of getting the three of them in and out of the camp without being seen or heard. He was an expert in using navigational equipment.

Lily had to listen to what the terrorist leaders were saying, memorize it and translate it when they got back to base.

If they got back.

Rob held the Squad in position, giving himself time to focus a pair of night-vision goggles. Now he could see the camp in perfect detail, everything green and clear, including three shapes lying motionless on the desert floor.

'Dogs,' he whispered to Lesh.

Lesh – shorter and stockier than Rob – nodded and directed his two friends to the north of the camp, changing direction because the wind was coming from the south and the dogs would be less likely to smell them if they came in from the north.

Ten minutes later, the three children were next to the tent, as planned, having crawled an exhausting last fifty metres on their stomachs, a manoeuvre known as the leopard crawl.

They had rehearsed this operation five times before, less than a hundred kilometres away at a replica camp. But that had been practice and this was for real.

You could never predict the kinds of things that might go wrong, however many times you practised. But, so far, nothing had gone wrong: no camel had groaned, no dog had barked, no guard had taken the safety catch off his gun. The desert was so quiet, in fact, that the noise of a plane flying overhead had distracted the guards, causing them to gaze up at its blinking lights. One guard pointed his gun at it, baring his teeth in a wide grin.

Rob smiled and put his thumb up to Lesh. He'd done his job. They were inside the camp and none of the guards had any idea they were there. Now Rob looked at Lily because the next bit was down to her.

Lily nodded – knowing what was required – and put her left ear against the fabric of the large tent, focusing quickly on the voices inside. She stuffed her blonde curls under a black hat, so that they didn't get in her way.

There were three men speaking Arabic in fast, low voices, but Lily could still understand every word. She had an amazing skill: she could speak dozens of languages. It was her life's ambition to learn every language in the world.

As she listened, Rob looked one way and Lesh the other. Both were squatting, covering every angle, alert to the high possibility of being discovered.

Lily knew she had to focus all her attention on the words coming from inside the tent, leaving everything else to Rob and Lesh.

'The hour is nearly upon us,' she heard one voice saying. Not a Saharan voice. Lily knew most Arab dialects and what she was hearing was not local to this part of North Africa. 'Soon,' the voice went on, 'we will have all of our people in position. Our attack will be irresistible. But first we must . . .'

At that moment the canvas of the tent caved in and snapped back painfully against Lily's ear.

Something had gone wrong. Terribly wrong.

Lily looked to her left to see Lesh, illuminated by the soft light coming from the tent, staring past her, his face tight with shock. So she turned to her right to see that Rob had fallen against the canvas and was now sprawled on the ground.

Rob had heard what he thought was a shrill alarm going off right next to him and had stumbled in shock against the tent. But it had been no alarm, just a tiny fly fizzing about inside his ear.

Loud voices broke the sudden silence.

Questions.

Orders.

Shouts from inside and outside the tent.

Without a word, the three children stood and ran at top speed, just as they had practised, making use of their special studded shoes to get a better grip on the loose sand. They knew exactly where they had to run: a fixed point one kilometre to the east. Their only chance of surviving.

Rob then shouted into a mic in his watch as he ran. 'Abort mission. Abort!'

Cracks of gunfire filled the air as rounds of ammunition came over their heads, accompanied by the thump of the guns. The glow of tracer rounds fizzed about them.

Lily was ahead of the others to start off with. She was a good runner, as well as being a gifted linguist. Her dad had taken her running on the hills where they used to live when she was very young.

They ran as fast as they could for one minute, then at half speed to conserve energy. Lily had played her part well. But had they got away? Should they go to ground? It was for Rob to decide. He had to keep his cool, even though he was painfully aware that it was his fault that everything had gone wrong.

Before Rob had a chance to make his mind up about what to do next, the trio was lit up from behind at the same time as they heard the scream of an engine.

'The Land Rover!' Lesh shouted.

Rob knew Lesh was right. It was the vehicle they had seen back at the camp. He remembered that it had been fitted with four headlamps above the windscreen. He had seen it through the night-vision goggles and grimaced at the irony that they were being hunted down by a vehicle that was made in the UK, the very country they were there to protect. He had no doubt that there would be a machine-gunner leaning out of its passenger window.

Now they were running at full speed again. It was exhausting and painful, but they had no choice.

Rob saw more red-hot tracer rounds skimming the sand dunes ahead of them. There were a dozen sounds to identify at once: guns, dogs, shouts, engines. It was impossible for his head to take it all in.

But then there was something else. A louder noise drowning out everything. Rob looked up instinctively, still running, to see something looming over them, something huge and black, so black it was darker than the sky. A double set of rotors were moving the air, the sand and everything in between.

Rescue in the form of a massive night-operational Chinook helicopter.

'Down!' Rob shouted. 'Down. Down. Daaaa . . .'

Lesh hit the ground, arms over his head, to avoid both the incoming fire and the sand the helicopter was whipping up. He knew exactly what the Chinook would do and that an Apache attack helicopter, armed with four Hellfire missiles, would be coming in as an escort. This was how the British army responded when a mission went wrong.

Although they were in an extremely dangerous situation, Lesh was thrilled by the military hardware that was hanging over them and by what it was about to do, and he felt a new explosion of adrenalin rushing through him as he grinned and cowered at the same time.

Lily squatted on the ground and put her hands over her ears, protecting herself, waiting to feel Rob crouch down next to her.

But Rob was not next to Lily.

She closed her eyes now because she knew what was coming. Two missiles from the Apache to stop the camp guards in their tracks, to buy the three of them time to get on to the Chinook, which was now touching down.

The missiles came a second later. *Whoosh. Thump. Whoosh. Thump.* Sand and shrapnel and pieces of Land Rover tossed across the desert floor, everything lit up by all the colours of the rainbow in a series of blinding flashes and pulses.

As the lights faded, the only sound Lily could hear was coming from the Chinook's rotor blades. A violent whirring.

Lesh lifted his head off the sand and looked back, waiting for Rob's order to board the Chinook. His mouth was full of sand and he could feel grains in his eyes and inside his clothes. But there was no word from Rob. All Lesh could hear was a muffled cry coming from near to where he knew their leader had last been.

Lily sat up. She had known instinctively what was wrong from the moment Rob had not crouched next to her. 'He's hit!' she yelled above the sound of the helicopter.

'Come on!' Lesh shouted back. 'I can see him.' He had spotted a shape in the sand ten metres away illuminated by the burning Land Rover, whose petrol tanks had just caught fire. They ran to what looked like a bundle of clothes twisted into a heap.

Rob.

On his back, holding his leg, his fingers grasping at a black-red hole the size of a tennis ball in his thigh. He was screaming with pain now.

Lily and Lesh hesitated. But only for a second. It was a shock to see Rob so terribly injured and in such agony, and they felt sick and frightened, but, over-riding all that, they felt calm. This was a job they'd been trained to do and they were going to do it.

Lesh and Lily each took one of Rob's arms over their shoulder, then they ran hard towards the back ramp that was coming down from the Chinook. A soldier, sitting at a fixed machine gun, moved out of the way to let them board. They fought through the whirring air and a billion particles of sand, on to the chopper.

Towards safety.

The pilot shouted, 'Lifting!' and immediately the Chinook was airborne, the sky and the desert floor swirling with stars and fires and bullets as the children sprawled on the bottom of the ascending aircraft.

Immediately a pair of medics leaped from the benches on either side of the Chinook's fuselage to treat Rob's leg, first tying a tourniquet round his upper thigh to reduce the blood loss, then giving him a massive injection of morphine to ease the pain.

Lily and Lesh looked to the far end of the helicopter and saw a figure studying them. She was dressed in a white jacket and skirt, her nails painted, her hair a perfect copper bob. She looked absurd in this terrifying setting, next to the medics dressed in regular army fatigues. It was as if she'd just stepped out of a smart London restaurant and wasn't in a helicopter that was screaming across the Sahara Desert.

Julia. Their commander.

'What happened?' she asked calmly, her eyebrows arched.

'They heard us,' Lily answered, gasping for air, glancing at Rob on the floor of the helicopter, where the two medics were now leaning over him, one with his hands on Rob's chest, pushing down in short, sharp jerks.

'How?' Julia pressed Lily. 'How did they hear you?'

'It went wrong,' Lesh coughed, not taking his eyes off Rob and the medics.

Then another voice filled the aircraft. The pilot over the speakers. 'We've got a choice now. We can either go smooth and slow, or fast and . . .'

'Fast!' one of the medics shouted. 'As fast as possible.'

AFTER THE FUNERAL

Five children emerged from a beautiful stone church set among fields in the English countryside. The sun blazed down on trees and hedges and birdsong, creating the perfect rural scene.

The children crossed a country lane and headed into a field of long grass that was baking in the heat, a church bell tolling every few seconds. Three hundred metres away, next to a half-collapsed barn, a woman was waiting for them. She was dressed all in white and her short copper-coloured hair shone in the sun.

Julia again.

The five children were wearing black and they all looked miserable.

A tall girl with long blonde ringlets. Lily.

A pale stocky boy wearing a black coat and a frown. Lesh.

A beautiful black girl wearing a flowery scarf. Hatty.

A short Asian boy with his hair shaved close. Adnan.

And the tallest, a good-looking tanned boy with brown hair. Kester.

The Squad, minus one, a week since their leader and friend, Rob, had died in the helicopter above the Sahara Desert.

They walked towards Julia without speaking. What could they possibly say? They had been trained to spy, to evade capture, to fool people into thinking that they were just ordinary children, but they had not been trained to deal with the death of one of their own.

They were all heartbroken.

Every government needs spies. In Britain there are two major organizations that use them.

The first – MI5 – keeps things safe at home. It protects the United Kingdom from people who want to cause chaos: bombers, thieves, kidnappers, terrorists and more.

The second – MI6 – looks out for threats coming from abroad. Countries that jeopardize the security of the UK government and its citizens. Individuals and groups from any of the world's other 196 countries that might want to attack, destabilize or steal from the UK.

The government directs MI5 and MI6, but some spies are special, so special that they need to be kept secret even from the government, from everyone apart from a small community of people who live to serve their country whoever is in charge.

The Squad.

These six – now five – children take orders from a handful of adult spies, but, apart from them, nobody knows who they are or what they do.

There is another thing that binds the Squad together. Something that happened two years ago and led directly to them becoming spies. A terrible, unimaginable, unforgettable day.

As she walked towards the barn, Lily was thinking about that day: the last time, before Rob, that she'd had to face the death of people she loved. She could remember it more clearly than she wanted to. It had been a summer day and all six children had been with their parents. They'd known each other since they were babies because some of their mums and dads worked together. They hadn't really known what work their parents did before that day, but now they all knew that their parents had been spies.

Lily stopped herself dwelling on that: she wanted to think about Rob.

In the week since his death she had felt restless and uneasy. This was the first time that someone from their unit had died. The shock was horrible. But this was what being a spy was really like. If adults spy, some will die. If children spy, some will also die.

Their handlers had kept them busy all week, taking them to the Lake District where they had carried out training in the woods, river-rafting, snorkelling; they'd even had them playing football. It had felt like a multi-sports week that a school might organize and the children hadn't been sure if they were being trained or being given things to do that would take their minds off the events in the Sahara Desert.

Lily had spent some of the time alone during the week. They all had. Adnan had gone off in his canoe for hours. Lesh had escaped to his room to work on his electronic devices.

Lily had chosen fell-running. The Lake District was perfect for that because the hills were so steep and wild and she could push herself. When she was on the tops of the hills, alone, she always felt as though her dad was running beside her.

'What's this about?' Adnan asked, looking at Lily and Lesh as they approached the farm building. 'Are we going to have a barn dance?'

Lily shrugged. As usual, Adnan wanted to get a laugh out of them to make them feel better, but it hadn't worked. Not this time. Lily was too worried about what they were about to be asked to do, trying to control her fear that they might have to go back to the desert.

'What?' Adnan asked again, rubbing his hand over his shaven head. 'Seriously. What is this about?'

'We don't know,' Hatty answered calmly, noting that Julia had disappeared into the barn.

'It's another mission, I'd guess,' said Kester,

pulling his black tie off and messing up his neat brown hair.

'But now?' Lily asked, sounding confused. 'After Rob? It can't be. It's too soon.'

'Lesh?' Kester asked. 'What do you think?'

Lesh had said nothing since leaving the church. He eyed his four friends, then breathed in. 'It's a mission,' he said in an almost inaudible voice. 'She's chosen the barn because no one will have bugged it and it'll be hard to follow us here. Not that anyone would. That means she wants to tell us something sensitive. This is the perfect spot for us to be given a new mission.'

Lily nodded: he was right. The Squad walked the rest of the way in silence.

The inside of the barn was dark compared to the brilliant light outside, but Julia stood out regardless, almost like she was glowing. There were bales of hay scattered on the floor and the children sat on them when Julia indicated they should, although she remained standing.

'We have to be quick,' Julia said. 'Listen.'

No one replied. No one dared. Even though ten minutes ago they'd been standing round an open grave, crying their eyes out, there was no question that they wouldn't be ready to go back to business straight away.

'Thank you,' Julia said, her voice softening. 'How was the funeral?'

Lily felt her eyes well with tears as Julia looked at her.

'I wish I could have been there,' Julia added.

Lily tried to smile. *It must be even harder for Julia*, she thought. As a known spy commander, Julia could never draw attention to herself by attending one of their funerals. Especially now that everyone seemed to know who all the adult spies were.

'Anyway.' Julia cleared her throat, her voice back to normal. 'As you know, it's Euro 2012 in three weeks.'

'Euro what?' Adnan asked.

'Euro 2012,' said Kester. 'The sixteen top national football teams in Europe play each other to find out who is best. It's being held in Poland and Ukraine.'

'With Poland walloping everyone in sight,' Lesh muttered, bringing a smile back to Lily's face.

'No way,' Lily said. 'Just pray that Poland don't have to play England until the final. And that's as far as you'll get.'

'Exactly,' Julia said. 'I mean that's exactly what Euro 2012 is. I suspect England will not get to the final though, Lily . . . Anyway, there's a bigger problem.'

'What's that?' Kester asked.

'We have strong intelligence that someone is planning to attack the England team in Poland.'

The children all spoke at once.

'What?'

'Who?'

'No way!'

'Well, that definitely means England won't get to the final,' Adnan muttered.

'We don't know who they are,' Julia explained, ignoring Adnan's joke. 'But we do know where they are.'

'And?' Hatty said.

Julia eyed Hatty before she went on. 'We've been monitoring a small group of men who are travelling on foot through Ukraine towards Poland, coming through woods and mountains, off-road, as if they're trying to conceal their approach. In addition, we have some intelligence – lifted from the Russians – that a threat to the England team could be emerging. We're thinking the two things are linked.'

'Who are these men?' Hatty asked.

'Possibly a terror group. Possibly from an Arab country,' Julia continued. 'We're not sure.'

'So how do we know they're not just hikers?' Kester asked.

'They're travelling over borders illegally. They're not moving on established paths. It's like they're trying to be invisible. Which – ironically – makes them stand out. Also they seem to be carrying some sort of military hardware.'

'So they're a possible threat and you want us to check them out?' Adnan asked.

'Yes. We want you to go in and – in a black op – do just that.'

'Black op?' Kester asked. 'Do you mean one that no one else knows about and that if we fail, we're on our own?'

'Yes,' said Julia gravely.

'So why us?' Hatty cut in. 'Why not leave them to the Russians?'

'This is a threat to British civilians, Hatty. We want to be in control.'

'So if the Russians know about a potential threat,' Hatty pressed, 'don't they know about these men?'

'As far as we know, they don't. As far as we know, no one is tracking them on foot or by satellite, or any other way. Except us. If we keep an eye on them, we can deal with the situation when we need to, and if we need to, without causing any diplomatic difficulties.'

'But why attack the England team?' Lily murmured, trying to work it out.

'They're high-profile,' said Julia. 'English Premier League players are the best known on the world stage. If our players are attacked, it will have a bigger impact across the world media and will therefore create more fear.'

'But still . . .' Lily said.

'We have to go with what we're hearing, Lily. It may be nothing; however, we have no choice but to follow it up. Ignoring this intelligence could be a deadly mistake.'

'And what do you want us to do about it?' Kester asked, standing up.

'We have to find out if this group is about to attack the England team or not and, if they are, when. They're travelling through the woods on foot by day and they camp at night in remote places. We need you to get near to them, so that you can gather intelligence.'

'How have you been tracking them?'

'Satellite,' Julia said, 'and we've had a drone on them.'

'A drone? Really?' Lesh jumped up, speaking for the first time. 'What kind of drone?'

Julia shrugged. 'I have no idea, Lesh. A small unmanned plane that takes photos from above and sees what is going on without being spotted. A drone!'

'Yes, but is it a Predator? Is it one of the modern ones? Is it a US drone or UK?'

'So why not send in the Special Forces?' Hatty broke in, glaring at Lesh, who always became excited about technology. 'Some adults at least.'

'That's a good question, Hatty.'

'But what's the answer?' Hatty snapped back, her dark eyes trained on Julia.

Julia frowned at Hatty for a moment, then went on. 'There's a youth football tournament involving an England team in Poland this week. A prelude to Euro 2012. It's in a town near the border with Ukraine. There's no way we can move the Special

Forces in there without the risk of them being identified. We need a way of getting our operatives in without anyone noticing. If we place the five of you in the youth team, who would suspect anything? You'll be very close. It's a perfect cover: you can play football by day and spy at night.'

'So that's why we've been playing football all week.' Lily pushed her blonde ringlets behind her ears. 'Great.'

'But I hate football,' Hatty snorted.

'Maybe you do, Hatty. However,' Julia added, raising her eyebrows, 'I suspect you're very good at it.'

'I'm good at everything.' Hatty smiled. 'Adnan – on the other hand – is not.'

Everyone looked at Adnan.

'I do hate football,' he said, trying to be honest. 'I mean, what's the point of a load of people running around chasing a bag of air and getting all excited when one of them kicks it past another into a net? It's pathetic. There's no discipline. Not like kickboxing. Mountaineering. Kayaking. They're proper sports. Football's for kids.'

'Yes, Adnan,' Julia said wearily. 'I might even agree with you. But is it true that you can't play?'

Adnan shrugged. 'I'm hopeless.'

'But I thought you were good at sport.'

'I am. Karate. Judo. Rafting. Climbing. I'm great with my hands.'

'But with your feet?'

'Less good.' Adnan grinned.

Everybody laughed. But it was hollow laughter because now they were thinking about their next mission and all the problems and dangers it would entail.

'Is this going to work?' Hatty asked. 'I mean, we can do a lot and we can do it well, but football?'

'We have no choice,' Julia answered. 'You know that. Two years ago all the adult spies were compromised. That's why . . . you know that was why your parents were caught out. Adult spies are good, but who is going to monitor children like you? You'll go under the radar. Using adults is still so risky.'

'But surely there are better options than us?' said Hatty.

'No, there are no better people than you,' Julia said. 'We've watched you all week and we think we can easily fit four of you into a team, with some coaching and tactical help, as the other footballers you'll be playing with are exceptional.'

'There are five of us,' Hatty said.

'Adnan's the weak link in this case,' said Julia. 'He admits that himself. But for the rest of the mission he's the strong link. You could be using a variety of insertion methods like marching through forests, rafting down difficult rivers and snorkelling. Any of these things. Tell me, Hatty, who do you want with you on those exercises?'

Hatty sighed. 'Adnan.'

'Right then.' Julia moved forward. 'I want Hatty and Kester to stay behind. The rest of you, back to the cars by the church.'

So Lily, Lesh and Adnan walked back out into the blinding light and heat of the fields, wondering what Julia had to say to Kester and Hatty that she couldn't share with them.

A DIFFICULT CHOICE

Through the barn door, Kester watched the others disappearing along a path of sun-bleached grass and tiny blue flowers. He had to squint because it was so bright outside the barn. When they were out of sight, he looked at Julia, who was gazing at him as if she was trying to make a decision.

'You know why I've kept you both back?' she asked, looking briefly at her red-painted finger-nails.

'Yes,' Kester and Hatty said at the same time.

'So who should it be? Who's going to be the new leader of the Squad?' Julia stood over them both. 'Hatty? What do you think?'

Hatty smiled, brushing some straw off her skirt. She knew Julia would ask her first. Julia was always pushing her, making it hard. So she decided to make it hard for Julia by answering her question with one of her own, something Julia herself had trained Hatty to do.

'Who's on the shortlist?' Hatty said.

Now it was Julia's turn to smile. 'Who do you think should be on the shortlist, Hatty?'

Kester had said nothing so far. He was quite enjoying watching Julia and Hatty jousting. But deep down he knew how he wanted this conversation to go. The question was who was going to be leader of the Squad? He wanted the answer to be Kester. He had wanted to be leader two years ago when they'd chosen Rob and he had said nothing. Rob had been the right person then. But Kester was more ambitious now. Saying that, he didn't want to push himself forward as leader: he wanted to be chosen because people thought he was the right person for the job.

'It's obvious,' Hatty said, replying to Julia's question. 'It's either Kester or me.'

'Why?' Julia asked.

Hatty looked at Kester. 'Kester has natural authority. The other three look up to him. They like him. They listen to him.'

'Do they listen to you, Hatty?'

'They do.'

'Kester?' Julia said. 'Who shouldn't be leader?'

Now Kester smiled. He liked the way Julia asked questions, trying to unsettle him. Not who should be leader, but who shouldn't.

'Adnan should not be leader,' Kester said. 'He has a lot of skills. He has superb survival knowledge and he can make us all laugh . . . But he's not a leader.'

'And Lesh?'

'Lesh is the same. His skills are so focused on surveillance technology that he needs to give that his all. He would hate to be leader.'

'And Lily?'

'Lily is intelligent and everybody loves her,' Kester went on. 'She's kind and nurturing and strong, but not tough-minded enough to lead. Her strengths lie in other places.'

'Hatty?'

Kester swallowed. Now he had to tell the truth – a truth that would not help his case. 'Hatty would make an excellent leader,' he said. 'She's decisive, calm, clear-thinking, intelligent and hard.'

'Hard?' Julia pressed. 'What do you mean?'

'She could make the right choice even in the most dangerous of circumstances.'

'And what about you, Kester? Would you make a good leader?'

Kester nodded, glancing at Hatty, whose face was expressionless. 'Yes, I would. And I want to be the leader.'

Julia turned to Hatty and paused. Outside the sun was still scorching the fields and the birdsong had died down as the day became even hotter. The church bell had stopped tolling after the funeral.

'Hatty? It's you or Kester. Who should I choose?'

'Don't you know?' Hatty asked her commander.

'I do,' Julia said, 'but I want you to make the decision, Hatty.'

Kester frowned at this. Why did Hatty get to choose? But he said nothing. He could feel his heart beating faster, so he calmed himself by breathing in and out more slowly.

Hatty had not answered the question yet. She looked at Kester and she looked at Julia.

'Do you think Kester would be a good leader?' Julia pressed.

'I do.'

'Better than you?'

'No,' Hatty said.

Hearing this, Kester closed his eyes. That was it. He'd lost. Again.

'But,' Hatty went on.

'But what?' Julia asked.

'But I think that, although I have superior leadership skills, the other three would respond better to Kester.'

Kester opened his eyes and stared at Hatty.

'Do you?' said Julia, sounding genuinely surprised. 'Why?'

'Because, like Kester says, I'm hard. But what he means by that is that I'm less likeable. There'll be times when the other three won't agree with the decisions their leader makes, and at that point I think they'd respond better to him than to me.'

'So you choose Kester?' Julia asked.

'I do,' Hatty said, staring hard at her friend.

Kester stared back at her, eye to eye, for what seemed like ages, until Julia stood between them and ordered them to follow the other three back across the fields towards the church.

'Come on,' she said. 'You've got work to do.'

FOREIGN LAND

The moment the five Squad members stepped outside the exit of Krakow's John Paul II International Airport in Poland, a large black people carrier with the England football crest on the door moved smoothly across the road and stopped next to them.

The people carrier was part of their cover: they were young footballers arriving for a tournament. That was why they were all wearing England tracksuits and carrying branded Umbro bags. All part of the cover.

Several adults and children stopped to look at them, nudging each other and pulling out smartphones to take photographs.

Lily forced herself not to look the other Squad members in the eye, knowing that she would smile or laugh if she did. They were living a bizarre fantasy, pretending to be England footballers in tracksuits, and she didn't want to blow their cover, however exciting it felt.

Hatty, on the other hand, was not happy to be wearing a football tracksuit. She hated it. She liked to wear fashionable tops and skirts and scarves and felt ridiculous. But she knew she had to shrug off those feelings and play her part so, to take her mind off that, she focused on the outside of the airport.

Any foreign county is marked by strange smells and signs and images. Hatty saw posters advertising products she'd never seen before using the different words and accents of the Polish language. There was a man frying sausages on what looked like a barbecue right outside the airport door. And next to the modern steel and glass airport were a forest and a tumbledown wooden farmhouse with chickens pecking outside. It was so unlike the airports in England that were characterized by motorways, endless car parks and glossy hotels.

One by one they hauled their bags into the vehicle. Kester was the last in, so he slid the door to and tapped on the glass for the driver to set off.

Hatty wanted to ask Lesh about the differences she'd noticed between home and this country. Lesh had been born in Poland, but had moved to England when he was very young. He would have some enlightening things to say and she wanted to hear them. But there was a quiet atmosphere in the people carrier as everyone put their safety belts on. Sensing that no one wanted to talk, Hatty decided to ask him later.

As the vehicle moved off, heading into central Krakow where they would be playing football and staying in a hotel, Hatty stared out of the tinted window to watch people walking to and from the airport.

'How was the flight?' a voice came over a speaker, breaking the silence. It was, of course, Julia. Hatty imagined her sitting at a desk in London, a cup of English tea on a saucer next to her, ready to give her orders.

'Great,' Kester said, speaking first.

'Not so great,' Adnan countered. 'You had to pay to use the toilet on the plane.'

'Why was that a problem?' Julia asked.

'Why?' Adnan raised his voice. 'You shouldn't have to have to pay to . . . do . . . a . . . a . . . you know what.'

Everyone laughed. But not Julia. Her voice was crisp and businesslike.

'Did Adnan cause trouble?' she asked.

'No more than usual,' Hatty replied.

'Good. Well, stand by because I need to brief you a little more before you arrive. I'll speak to you again in five minutes.'

The vehicle was well away from the airport by now, taking them towards Krakow and they chatted as they passed castles on wooded hillsides and beautiful timber churches. Driving on the right, not the left, always made Hatty feel uneasy. She also noticed that every other lamp post had a Euro 2012 banner hanging off it. She had seen similar posters and banners in the airport.

'Do you think we'll be able to stay on to watch Euro 2012?' Lesh asked her, his face lit up with excitement.

'I hope not,' Hatty replied.

Lesh frowned, but said nothing.

As they waited to hear from Julia, Hatty took the chance to study Kester. He smiled back at her, but there was something in his smile that wasn't a hundred per cent confident.

He's not sure he should be leader, Hatty thought. *Maybe*.

She wondered why. It was probably because this was his first mission as leader. But it could also be that there were things about this mission that worried him, like how they could pretend they were footballers. Especially Adnan. That was the real problem that could undermine their cover.

Soon they were entering the city, with its tall buildings, traffic jams and people queuing at pedestrian crossings. Again Hatty observed the scene and tried to make sense of it as it rushed by. There were beautiful buildings that looked like churches and palaces next to really run-down grey office blocks covered in scrappy posters. It was like a rich country and a poor country had been mixed together at random.

'Right. Time to talk. Have you got the scrambler

on?' Julia's voice broke the sleepy feeling inside the people carrier.

Without another word, Kester took a small device – which looked exactly like an iPhone – out of his pocket. In fact, it was an iPhone, but it could do so much more. They all had one and called them SpyPhones as a joke. But essentially that's what they were: phones that helped them to spy, with several extra apps. The kind of apps most iPhone users could only dream about, from coding and decoding messages, opening electronically secured doors, X-ray and night-vision viewfinders and, when needed, they could even electrocute an enemy.

Kester flicked the scrambler switch on his SpyPhone. This meant no one would be able to listen in to their conversation using bugs or any other monitoring devices. It worked by filling the air around them with pulses of radio waves that would break up the signal to any known listening device. It was just another precaution. Although they were there under the cover of being young footballers, there was always a chance that someone was monitoring them.

'Ready,' said Kester.

'OK,' Julia started. 'We need to talk about the mission.'

On the plane, all five had already studied a series of encrypted documents that Julia had sent to their SpyPhones. As a result, they knew their mission in Poland had two objectives.

First, to gather evidence on the suspected terror group and whether an attack on the England team was being planned. This would involve anything from marches through woods at midnight to using devices to gather intelligence.

Second, to play in a young English football team in a tournament against countries from across Europe.

'So . . . any questions?' Julia asked as the people carrier drove along the bank of a river, beside rows of large and impressive buildings.

Adnan went first. 'How are we going to deal with the . . . the big problem?'

Julia paused. 'What big problem, Adnan?'

'That we've not played football at this level,' Hatty cut in.

'It's not ideal . . .' Julia began.

'It's not ideal?' Hatty raised her voice, glad to have a chance to get her worries off her chest. 'I know we're well prepared for what we usually do, but pretending to be really good footballers: that's a hard one to pull off.'

But Julia had an answer for Hatty. 'Has anyone heard of Jim Sells?'

Lily smiled and leaned towards the speaker. 'England defender. Played for West Ham, Leeds and Spartak Moscow.'

'Very good,' Julia said. 'Any more?'

'Central defender. Would do anything to stop the

opposition scoring. At the heart of England's defence for a decade. Now a freelance coach working with teams like Real Madrid and Zenit St Petersburg. He can turn a catastrophic backline into the best defence in Europe.'

'That's right,' Julia said. 'Well done, Lily. And that's exactly why he's going to be working with you.'

'No,' Lily gasped.

'Yes.'

'Awesome,' said Kester.

'Jim who?' Adnan asked.

'Sells,' Lily answered.

'So why is he working with us?' Hatty asked. 'We're kids.'

'We need someone who can make you excel. And quickly. You need to be convincing as footballers – or your mission won't work. Whatever Jim says, you do it. His word is final. OK?'

'What about the existing players?' Hatty asked. 'I take it we're replacing five of their former teammates and that they'll hate us for it.'

'That's right,' Julia replied, a stiffness in her voice. 'It will be very difficult.'

Hatty nodded, even though Julia could not see her. Then something else occurred to her. 'About Jim Sells?' she asked.

'Yes?'

'Will he know about our actual mission?' But Hatty already knew the answer to this. He would have to know. There was no way all this could happen without Jim Sells being involved in both the football *and* the spying.

They heard Julia clear her throat. 'Jim Sells has also worked for the government,' she said. 'He played football in Russia and, while there, did some special . . . favours for us.'

'Ahhh,' Lily said. 'That makes sense.'

'Jim Sells will be your commander in Poland. You do what he says on and off the field. Now we don't have long. Any more questions?'

Kester spoke next. 'How are the teams chosen for this tournament? It's clearly not players with teams like Chelsea and Liverpool – proper academy teams at professional clubs. So how does it work?'

'It's boys and girls of high ability,' Julia explained. 'But not ones attached to professional clubs. Amateurs, if you like.'

It was clear to the Squad what their job was. And it was clear it was not going to be easy. Even before they monitored the terrorists or whoever they were, they had to convince some of the country's best young footballers that they were great footballers too.

And they had to be ready to do it now because the car had stopped in the shadow of an impressive football stadium.

SPY FOOTBALLER

The full England youth team – including the five members of the Squad – were brought together in a function room high in the Wisła Stadium, overlooking the pitch.

In the room there were several round tables, fancy crystal chandeliers and framed pictures of Polish footballers on the walls. Hatty was intrigued by the Polish labels on the beer pumps and the water bottles. She still couldn't get her head round the unfamiliar words and wished she was as clever at languages as Lily.

Hatty watched as Kester led by example, going over to shake hands with all the real footballers. Lily, Adnan and Lesh joined him immediately. This was their first task: to settle into the team, to be friendly and open so that the other players didn't feel threatened. If they couldn't fit in and convince the others that they really were footballers, then their cover and the mission would have no chance.

They'd all been given name tags, which made

introductions easier. But someone had to observe as well, so Hatty stood back, watching the exchanges. Observation was something she'd got from her mother, who used to take her into town and sit in a cafe and people-watch. That's what she called it. She used to ask Hatty what she thought people were doing. Did anyone look like they were lost? Were any of them shoplifters or thieves? Were people kind or unkind? Hatty's mum had taught her a lot. But that was before the attack. *A lifetime ago*, Hatty thought.

Hatty noted which of the footballers was smiling genuine smiles – and who was faking. She knew there could be trouble. There were always difficulties when one group infiltrated another. It was human nature. Especially when one set were imposters like them. Hatty's priority was to anticipate who might feel threatened or, worse, guess that the Squad weren't who they claimed to be.

One boy stood out for Hatty. He was tall, black and athletic and seemed to have an energy that dominated the room. One of those people who everyone was aware of and everyone seemed to defer to. His name was Rio. Hatty wondered if he really was called that or if he'd somehow changed his name in homage to Rio Ferdinand, the England defender.

Then Hatty noticed two more who worried her. The first was a thickset lad called Finn. *Another stupid name*, she thought unkindly. She worked out quickly that he was a slavish follower of Rio. He laughed when Rio joked. He frowned when Rio was cross. The rest of the time he just stood there with a blank look on his face.

Then there was one of the girls. Georgia was her name. She was tall with long blonde hair and wore make-up and a constant smile. However, it was not a convincing smile. Georgia was standing next to Rio, but not really listening to him. She was too busy looking around. Looking at Kester mostly. And snatching glances back at Hatty.

A loud voice interrupted the chatting, the tense circling and making friends.

'Would everyone sit down, please?'

The voice was a man's. Loud, but not shouting. Strong, but not aggressive. Within five seconds, everyone was sitting quietly facing him.

'My name is Jim Sells,' the man said. 'Welcome to Poland.'

Jim was muscular, over six foot tall, had very short brown hair and not a bit of fat on him. He looked a bit like an Action Man.

'I should explain,' he smiled. 'For this tournament I'm your coach.'

There was a quiet unrest among the established footballers when he said this. Voices muttered between them. Hatty heard the boy called Finn say the word 'Geoff'. But she was also aware that because they knew that Jim Sells was a former England player, no one was daring to challenge him.

'I know this is a surprise,' Jim said, raising his voice a little, 'especially to those who've been in the team for a while, but your regular coach, Geoff Graham, has had to return to the UK on family business. They were hoping that replacing him with me – however temporarily – would help. If you don't know me, I'm a former England international and I've coached teams like Real Madrid and – '

Then a voice from the players interrupted him. Rio. 'We know who you are, Jim . . . er, Mr Sells. And we're big fans. But why has Geoff taken half the team with him too?'

Jim smiled. 'First, please call me Jim. Second, yes, several of the players have been kept in England as they are at a sensitive time with their education and family life. So I'd like to introduce and welcome a new draft of players.' Jim eyed the back row. 'I know you'll all get along fine.'

No one said anything for a moment. Then Georgia, the girl with long blonde hair, spoke up. 'With respect, Jim, we've not heard much about this before and there are only a couple of days to go before the tournament and . . .'

'I accept that and I apologize,' Jim said. 'This is not ideal. But to make it all more palatable for you I've arranged that – if we get to the final – the England first team will come to see you play . . .'

'Wow.'

'Really?'

'Amazing!'

A cacophony of excited voices silenced all dissent.

'And,' Jim went on, 'you'll all get to meet them. Now is everyone happy?'

'Yes!' several voices said at once. The atmosphere of the room had changed.

'Good,' said Jim.

As Jim talked, Hatty watched Georgia leaning forward more and more. She tried to spot a reflection of the other girl's face in one of the windows, but couldn't catch her expression. *And how's Rio taking the information?* she wondered. Was the news about meeting the England team enough of a distraction for him or would he still see the new players as a challenge?

'Our first game is against the Faroe Islands,' Jim pressed on. 'The best start we could have hoped for.' He went on to explain how the competition worked. There were eight teams competing. There would be a first round, two semi-finals and a final. If England beat the Faroe Islands, they would be through to play Poland or Spain in the semi-final.

'I hope you're all going to get along,' Jim concluded. 'I've already been working hard with the new players. They're going to form the defensive line, bearing in mind who the team has lost. I've been doing extra defensive coaching with them in England. They'd never played together or met before this week, but we're all confident, aren't we, kids?'

Kester, Lesh, Lily and Adnan all nodded eagerly. After a second, Hatty joined in, even though, like the others, she was not clear about everything that Jim was saying. But they were stuck with Julia's orders that Jim was their new commander.

Jim's talk had raised some questions for Hatty though. She wanted to know more about him. She knew that Julia had said he was on their side, but she never trusted anyone at first. They had to prove themselves.

Jim Sells interrupted Hatty's thoughts. 'OK, everyone, this was just a short hello. I want you to settle into the hotel next to the stadium. You're staying there with the other teams. I'd like you all on your best behaviour. You're representing your country. Tomorrow morning we'll train together for the first time. Eleven a.m. OK?'

The Squad gathered in Kester's hotel room immediately after dinner. They swept the room for bugs and other devices – a routine of checking light bulbs, picture frames and electrical equipment – then sat on the chairs and sofas that filled the room, taking in the fancy wallpaper and large pieces of polished furniture.

The Squad had stayed in all sorts of accommodation before: in palaces, monasteries and ordinary hotels. They'd also stayed in holes in the ground and on exposed mountain tops. This was, for Hatty, quite a luxurious hotel, except that the corridors weren't lit so you had to feel your way along the walls at times. But Hatty was aware that new countries always threw up unusual details that you could never make up.

Overall, Hatty felt uneasy. But she knew that was good: the more ill at ease she felt, the less detail she would miss on this mission and the better spy she could be.

Kester took out his SpyPhone and flicked the scrambler. The group instinctively huddled into a two-metre circle within the phone's range. Kester also put the TV on loud to make sure no one could listen at the door or through a wall. Before he spoke, he breathed in. He was the leader of the Squad now, replacing Rob. This was the first full discussion he was having to lead and he wanted to get it absolutely right.

'We need to talk about Jim,' he said quietly.

'We do,' Hatty agreed.

'I like him,' said Lily, smiling.

'Lily, you like everyone,' Hatty sneered. She had known Lily for years, but she still could not understand how the girl could be so nice and friendly all the time. Did she have no dark thoughts?

'What's wrong with that?' Lily frowned.

'We need to ask ourselves questions about everyone,'

Kester broke in, trying to regain control of the conversation. 'Even the people who are on our side. If Julia gives us someone to work with, we should trust them, but we should suss them out too, just in case.'

'Go on then,' Hatty challenged him. 'Ask a question.'

'Who is he?'

'A former England footballer,' Adnan answered. 'For what it's worth.'

'I think that's worth a lot,' Lily argued. 'He played for England for ten years and in three World Cups. He was famous for being passionate on the pitch. How much more could someone do to show they were patriotic?'

'But he's more than a footballer, isn't he?' Kester claimed.

'A former spy,' said Adnan. 'Our commander now.'

'What else?' Kester asked.

Lily pushed her SpyPhone in front of everyone, showing a picture from the Internet of Jim Sells in a West Ham top. 'It's definitely him,' she said.

Hatty decided it was time to ask her question. 'So how come . . .'

A loud triple knock on the door silenced her.

Nobody spoke.

Nobody moved.

'It's Jim,' a voice said. 'I think it's time you put your lights out. I'm taking the five of you for some special training tomorrow – and it'll be hard. Meet me at the stadium at nine sharp.'

The Squad stayed quiet for a moment, then Adnan asked the question that was on all of their minds.

'Do you think he heard all that?'

TRAINING

The Squad stood on the centre circle inside the empty Wisła Stadium. It was 9 a.m. and they'd already had breakfast.

They gazed around at the hoardings advertising Polish beers and TV stations. *Everything seems different from England,* Lily thought. *Even the grass and the colour of the sky.*

'OK, kids,' Jim said. 'I've brought you here for some extra training that no one needs to know about. But, before that, I think you have some questions for me. Please ask anything you like.'

There was a silence in the stadium as the five children looked at Jim. Where should they start?

Lily went first. 'We've been briefed in full about the mission,' she said tentatively. 'By Julia, but –

'But who exactly are you and what do you have to do with us?' Hatty cut in.

Lily put a hand to her forehead. Sometimes her friend's direct questions embarrassed her.

Jim cleared his throat quietly, then spoke. 'Can I

handle Hatty's question first please, Lily? I think it'll help.'

'Sure,' Lily smiled.

'In brief,' he said slowly. 'I'm Jim Sells. I used to play football for England, West Ham and some other clubs. I was a defender. Now I coach defending across the world.'

'And you played in Russia?' Hatty said.

'During my career I played for Spartak Moscow, yes.'

'And that's got something to do with why you're here with us?' Hatty pressed.

'I hope Julia told you about that,' Jim said, smiling. 'As a result of playing in Russia, I was recruited by the UK government to spy on the Russians.'

'Weren't you scared?' Kester asked. 'Going from football to this.'

'Yes, I was scared,' Jim said. 'But like you, I believe in my country. I don't have any children or a wife, so I don't have greater responsibilities – and I'm not a religious man. And, well, it felt exciting to be honest.'

Hatty understood that. 'Thank you.'

'You're welcome, Hatty. Now Lily?'

'When are we going on our first mission?' Lily asked. 'And how?'

'Good question,' Jim replied, dropping his voice. 'Tonight. We'll drop you into Ukraine once the target – the possible terrorists – is stationary.'

'Tonight?' Adnan said too loudly, his voice echoing off the stadium sides.

'Yes,' Jim said, soft-voiced.

'How will we get there?' Kester asked. 'It's a long way, isn't it? Or have they moved closer?'

'It's still a fair distance,' Jim said. 'But not by helicopter.'

Lily glanced at Lesh who she knew would already be grinning. He loved helicopters. He had a huge smile on his face.

'We've had some briefing notes,' Kester said. 'Maps, and so on. But they're vague. Do we know all we need to know?'

'No,' Jim replied. 'But, once the target has stopped tonight and we've assessed the terrain, we'll give you diagrams, pictures. But really that's why we need you in there. To find out all you can about the terrain, the men and their capabilities. You know pretty much everything I can tell you until tonight. So shall we do some training? I mean football training.'

The training began with a surprise. Jim fitted them all with an earpiece: the kind they might use on a mission. Then he told them what he wanted them to do.

'I want you to spread out across the width of the pitch, like a defence would in football. Then I want you to run as one, mid-pace, keeping a straight line. All five of you. Every few seconds I will speak to one of you through your earpiece, telling you to change

47

direction. Your job is to watch each other and respond so you stay in perfect line. OK?'

The first five minutes were a debacle. When one of them turned to run the other way, one, or even all of the others, would carry on the way they were going. It looked terrible, but that made them focus and, as a result, they stopped making so many mistakes and became more aware of each other. Twenty minutes in, they had it sorted, working better as a unit, barely missing a turn, all of them grinning.

And, because it was going so well, Lily let her mind go, like she did when she was running on the fells at home, no longer controlling her emotions or keeping a grip on her thoughts.

Her first thought was that this football training was like preparing for a mission. Trying something again and again, making mistakes, overcoming them and improving. Whatever they did, it worked like this: making a shelter in a South American rainforest, following suspects on the streets of London, target shooting practice.

Lily frowned suddenly. Memories came back to her: of the day that they were recruited, of the day their parents had been murdered.

All the Squad members' parents were spies and, because they all knew each other, the kids had grown up going camping together to a place in the Lake

District twice a year. Tents. Boats. Fishing. Outdoor stuff. As the children got older, they started challenging the adults to competitions. Who could catch the most fish. Giant treasure hunts across mountain tops. Then, on the day it all changed, raft building.

The challenge that day was to build a raft big enough to get all their team across the lake to an ice-cream shop on the other side of the water. Kids versus adults.

Both teams had started building their rafts, using material from the woods that ran to the edge of the water by the campsite. But when the kids' raft was ready they saw that the adults weren't even half done. They'd been messing about, maybe even losing on purpose. So, with the adults still on the beach, the children were already halfway across the lake.

Lily had been the first to see it.

The sound of gunfire reached them across the smooth surface of Lake Ullswater at the same time as she said, 'There's something happening on the beach . . .' That was all she had been able to say. Then the six children – aged eleven then – had seen a group of ten masked men emerging from the woods at the side of the water, all bearing machine guns, all firing, pieces of wood and stones flying around, their parents falling.

The government did everything they could do look after the six orphaned eleven-year-olds. They assigned them an adult, who was a senior spy herself, to look after all their needs as they tried to rebuild their lives without parents.

But it became clear to the children that there could be no rebuilding.

They could never go back. There was nothing to go back for.

They would have to go forwards.

They approached the senior spy looking after them – a woman called Julia – with an idea. Rather than be mollycoddled as damaged children, protected from everything, they could become protectors themselves, using their status as children to go to places and find out things that adult spies never could.

At first, Julia had dismissed the idea, but the next day she came back to them and agreed to it.

And there was a good reason.

The entire network of British spies across the world had been compromised. No British spies were secret any more. The attack on their parents had been a result of that security breach. It was an emergency that needed a radical solution.

Six children became part of that solution: no one would expect spies to be under sixteen.

Lily heard voices calling her and she realized that she had stopped running, stopped training and was standing in the middle of the pitch, staring at the grass in a trance. She looked up to see five boys coming towards them across the pitch.

'Who are they?' she asked Hatty.

'Wisła's youth team. Under-elevens apparently,' Hatty explained.

'And why are they here?'

'They're going to attack,' Jim said. 'And you are going to defend.'

Jim had arranged for five Wisła youth team members to come and play attack-and-defence against the Squad. But they weren't thirteen-year-olds like the Squad: they were all aged ten.

Jim set up a defence with Lily and Lesh in the middle, Hatty on the left and Adnan on the right. Kester was in goal.

'Why am I in goal?' he asked.

'Because you used to be a keeper,' Jim said.

'How did you know that?'

'I know a lot,' said Jim.

The game began. Badly. It took the under-elevens no time to find out the Squad's weakness. After the Polish boys got their third goal, Lesh heard them talking. Up to this point he had loved playing against a Polish team. It was nice to hear them shouting in his first language. But not any more.

'Are these really England players? They're a joke.'

'They're older than us too. They're rubbish.'

Adnan was next to Lesh and Lily as Kester was picking the ball out of the net. 'What are they saying?' he asked.

'Nothing much,' Lesh replied glumly.

'Go on,' Adnan insisted. 'I bet they're proud to be playing the mighty England, aren't they?'

'It's something like that, Adnan,' said Lily.

By the time the Wisła players had reached nine goals, Adnan was losing it. He knew he was the weak link and that the others had actually done quite well, even Kester, who had made a couple of good saves.

As soon as Jim blew his whistle to give the players a rest, Adnan went over to him.

'Drop me,' he said. 'I'm rubbish.'

Jim smiled. 'Adnan. I can't.'

'Why not?' Adnan protested.

'Why do you think?'

Lesh leaned forward. He knew the answer. 'Because Adnan is an expert river-rafter and scuba-diver. Because we were practising both activities in England, meaning there's a good chance we'll be doing them out here. That's why we need him. And if he's part of the mission, that means he needs to be part of the team too.'

'Exactly,' Jim said.

The game restarted. There was a cool breeze blowing across the pitch now and Adnan felt it keenly, upset that he was letting everyone down.

When a boy a foot shorter took the ball around him for the twelfth time, then passed it back to a teammate, Adnan felt at fault. He saw the Wisła player lining up a shot. And he couldn't control himself. If he wasn't going to stop them with his feet, he'd have to do something else. He was determined to prevent another goal, whatever it took. So, as the shot came in, he leaped off the floor and caught the ball in his hand. It was an amazing catch. The way he'd reached out. His agility. His reflexes. All down to his martial arts training – and completely illegal.

There was a moment of silence before the young Polish players began to complain.

'Penalty!' They even shouted it in English. And it was a penalty.

Adnan watched the boy whose shot had been handled pick up the ball and put it on the spot.

Kester rubbed his gloves together and crouched. He was determined to stop this one. The score was 9–0 and double figures would be embarrassing. Then he heard a voice coming from behind the goal.

'Kester. Swap with Adnan.'

'What?'

'I want Adnan in goal now. You go right back.'

Kester knew to do exactly what Jim asked without looking upset. He had to make it look like it was normal, so he handed the goalkeeping gloves to Adnan.

'Go in goal,' Kester muttered.

'I've never played in goal in my life,' Adnan argued.

Kester shrugged.

Jim had made it over to them by now. 'That was a fine catch, Adnan. Your reflexes are great. That's down to your martial arts skills I expect.'

'What's it got to do with martial arts?'

'When the ball comes at you, pretend it's an arm attacking you. You've got superb reflexes. You're tall. You're athletic. You move like a cat. You're a natural keeper.'

Adnan shrugged, then pulled the gloves on and stood a couple of metres in front of the goal, waiting for the penalty to be taken. The player at the penalty spot put his hands out, complaining.

'You need to be on the goal line,' Lily told Adnan in a soft voice.

Adnan walked backwards. Then, remembering what Kester had done, he crouched and eyed the ball.

The penalty taker smiled and stepped up to hit a shot hard and low which skimmed the grass towards the bottom right corner. The perfect penalty.

But Adnan was in the air diving, his arm outstretched, his fingertips reaching as the ball was about to speed over the line, pushing it round the post.

The perfect penalty – but an even more perfect save.

Adnan heard Jim's huge hands clapping first. Then his teammates shouting and cheering. They'd found a role for Adnan.

FIGHT

The youth tournament organizers had arranged for a place in the hotel where the young players could relax away from the public eye: it had a drinks machine, sofas, a table football game and a pool table.

The Russian players were sitting at one end of the room, an adult talking to them in a quiet voice, occasional laughter breaking out.

The England players were standing round the drinks machine and the pool table. None of the Squad felt like being there. They wanted to be in bed. In two hours they were heading off to Ukraine for their first mission, but Jim had insisted that they mix with the other players, to make friends and try to fit in.

Kester was talking to one of the original team, Johnny, who was reading a book.

'What are you reading?' he asked, having already spotted it was *Stormbreaker*, a favourite book of his.

'Alex Rider,' Johnny replied. 'It's a spy story. I love books like this.'

Kester smiled, then, to cover his reaction, said, 'They're by Anthony Horowitz, aren't they? I love them too.'

'Do you?' Johnny said enthusiastically. 'What else do you like?'

'The Young Bond series,' Kester said. 'H.I.V.E. Lots of series like those.'

'Wouldn't you just love to be a spy?' Johnny said, an excited look on his face.

Kester felt like saying, 'No, it's really irritating. You never get any sleep,' but he thought better of it and nodded, mirroring Johnny's enthusiasm.

'Yes,' he answered. 'I would.'

Immediately he felt a hand on his shoulder and was worried that Jim had overheard him talking about spies.

'What about table football?' The voice was Rio's. 'Do you like that too?'

Kester turned and smiled. 'I love table football,' he said, knowing Rio was challenging him to a game.

'But are you any good?' Rio asked.

'I'm OK,' Kester replied. 'Sometimes I win. Sometimes I lose.'

'That's where you and me are different then.' Rio stared hard at Kester. 'I play to win.'

There was a silence. Kester wondered if he was supposed to feel scared at this point. 'Shall we?' he said at last. Rio grinned.

As Kester walked over to the table, he could sense

a change in the room: conversations tailing off, the sound of drinks cans being put down. He was trying to work out what was the best thing to do: win and face more animosity from Rio, or let him win and hope that they could become friends if Rio felt he had put one over on Kester.

Kester's mum and dad would have said win, win at all costs, win every point in every game. But Kester had never been like that. He could lose a battle if it meant they would win the war. He thought that if they'd been alive, his parents might have understood that now.

Kester decided that would be his strategy. Lads like Rio needed to feel that they were the best, then they relaxed. So he pretended he was rubbish at table football. He spun the players and clattered the ball in random directions. He could see it was working because Rio was grinning even more now and everyone had gathered round to see how truly great he was at table football.

Now that they were watching, Kester let Rio score. 0–1.

Georgia and Finn clapped wildly, but Kester noticed they were the only ones who did. So were the others in the team not so keen on Rio?

Rio was oblivious to that as he plucked the ball from the hole and kissed it, smirking at Kester. That was the point when something snapped in Kester's mind. He knew he should stay in control and calm, that this was only a stupid game with a stupid boy, but he hated bad winners more than he hated bad losers. Why should he let Rio win? So Kester decided *he* would win. He wasn't going to do it in an openly aggressive way, but he was going to win all the same.

The ball was on the table again, Rio hitting it hard, smashing it at Kester's goal over and over. No control. Just force. And quickly Rio scored a second one, rattling it in before Kester had a chance to gain control.

0–2.

Georgia and Finn clapped excitedly again and Rio grabbed the ball and kissed it. Again.

Kester could feel a rage coming on now. Everyone thought he was a calm and easy-going boy, that he never got flustered. But he did: he was just very good at hiding it. He knew he had to stop feeling angry and start taking control, so he breathed deeply to slow his heart rate down.

The ball clattered back into play. Now that Kester had calmed himself, he could feel his touch was just right. This was better. He used a defender to angle the ball to his midfield. Then a midfielder to angle it to a striker. Then he tapped it to the side with one striker and slammed the ball in with another.

Easy.

1–2.

Kester didn't look at Rio's face. He didn't kiss the

ball or smirk when he scored his second, third, fourth and fifth goals. All he did was focus, control the ball, move it around, shoot and score. No showing off. No posturing.

5–2.

When Kester got his sixth goal, he glanced up at Rio for the first time. He could tell immediately what was going to happen: Rio's fist was going to come across the table.

And he was right. Kester drew back to shift his balance, leaving the fist flailing to his left and Rio sprawling over the table. Kester heard screaming from the other England players, Hatty and Lily's voices, shouts from the Russians. Shouts that sounded like encouragement, like they were enjoying seeing the England players fight each other.

Kester stared at Rio and – keeping his voice calm as his attacker brushed himself down – asked, 'Do you want to finish the game?'

Rio snorted, his eyes wild and uncontrolled, then lunged again, both hands grabbing at Kester's shoulders. Kester countered the move by lifting his own arms and pushing them outwards, using a martial arts defence Adnan had taught him. An easy way to deflect such an attack.

This was OK. Kester could predict Rio's moves even before Rio had thought them up. No one was going to get hurt here. Rio was about to throw another punch, when a loud voice cut through it all.

'Stop!'

The room immediately went quiet. Jim was standing in the doorway. He did not look happy. He looked even less happy when the entire Russian team, including their coach, started clapping sarcastically.

Jim indicated, with two sharp jerks of his hand, that Kester and Rio should join him in the corridor. The two boys followed the former England international out of the room.

'I'm sorry, Jim,' Kester said, before their coach had spoken, hoping to make it easy for him. 'It was my fault. I got overheated.'

Then he saw Rio nodding, but not looking in Kester's eyes.

'I'm not going to blame one of you: I blame both of you,' Jim started. 'Did you see the Russian team in there, laughing at you? Remember, you're representing your country. I represented my country eighty-two times and I never showed indiscipline like that. What on earth is wrong with you?'

'Sorry, Jim,' Rio said. 'It won't happen again.'

'Sorry, Jim,' said Kester again.

'It'd better not happen again,' Jim finished. 'You can tell all the others this: any more incidents of any kind and I will come down hard on you.'

NIGHT VISION

It was dark when the Squad left through a fire exit, passing from the comfortable world of hotel rooms and fights about stupid things like table football into another world altogether. This was the kind of world most thirteen-year-olds would only read about in storybooks.

Their first objective was to cross a hundred metres of hotel lawn to the woods – woods that went on for hundreds of kilometres over rivers, over mountains and over borders.

They were dressed in T-shirts, jackets, cargo pants and boots. This was a night operation, so everything had to be black with no logos and no reflectors. Once they were clear of the hotel lawns, they stopped to smear camouflage cream on their faces, streaks of brown and green and black. They checked their earpieces and the small microphones set into their watches.

Finally Kester asked them all to jump up and down to make sure none of their kit was rattling. It wasn't: they'd done a good job preparing as usual.

They did all this in absolute silence, knowing exactly what they had to do.

Kester smiled once they were ready. How many times had they prepared themselves like this in training? Hundreds? But how many times had they been on real missions? Maybe a dozen? He was smiling because, when it was a mission, their adrenalin was always sky-high. You could train all you liked for the things you needed to do, but never for the way you would feel when it was real.

Kester looked back through the trees at a row of lit windows; they had left lights on timers in their bedrooms to give the impression that they were still in there, settling down for the night like normal children.

But they were not normal children at all.

Kester had that at the front of his mind as he faced the Squad. This was another big moment for him. He had been made leader and now he needed to show that he was strong and could make good decisions when they were on a mission. They had to trust him. It was easy to be a leader in hotel rooms and on football pitches, but would he be as decisive and focused when all of their lives were in danger? They were about to get on the helicopter. He needed to say something now, something that would chime with what they were all thinking.

'We all know that this is our first mission without Rob,' he said, looking at Lesh and Lily. 'And I know we're all thinking of him. Yes, I sound soft, but I feel that Rob is here, like he's looking out for us, that he would want us to go on. No question.'

Adnan smiled, about to speak, but managed this time to keep his joke to himself.

'That is soft, Kester,' Hatty agreed. 'But it's a good thought.'

None of the five spoke for a moment. In fact, they all seemed to have bowed their heads, as if in prayer.

After pausing, Kester slung his rucksack on to his back. He was ready to go. No more need for words. It was time for action.

The mission Jim had described to them sounded simple.

One, they had to walk into the Polish woods to reach a helicopter that would take them over the border into Ukraine.

Two, they would then be set down on the far side of a hill, six kilometres away from where the target appeared to be camping for the night.

Three, they had to hike to the camp and gather evidence without being seen.

The drone had been over the target in the last hour. Lesh had analysed its findings. It had picked up the heat from three bodies, none of them moving around, suggesting they were asleep. Probably.

'Just watch out for wolves,' Jim had said, making Adnan laugh.

'I mean it,' Jim said. 'Stay together and you'll be fine. They don't attack groups.'

Nobody saw Hatty shiver at that: she hated wolves, she always had.

The Squad had no control over the drone that Jim had referred to, but they did have a few gadgets. Gadgets to help them in case something went wrong. All five of them had night-vision goggles, which meant they would be able to see a hundred times better in the dark. As a group, they had GPS receivers, a SpyPad (both carried by Lesh), pin-sized tracking devices that they could attach to people or objects. In addition, they were wired to each other through a closed radio system, each with a mic on their watch and an earpiece.

One thing they would not have out in the field was radio contact with Jim, to make sure that they or Jim could not be listened into and, therefore, compromised.

After a light jog through the woods from the hotel, using the SpyPad to navigate, the Squad found the helicopter easily. To Kester's surprise, it wasn't a normal military transport helicopter, like a Chinook, but a medium-sized sleek black machine. They clambered aboard.

'What kind of helicopter is this?' Lesh asked, leaning towards the pilot.

The pilot grinned and tapped his nose. 'What helicopter?' he said.

'Wow,' Lesh whispered. 'This is . . . this is the secret chopper I've heard about . . . but no one has ever seen it . . . it goes under radar and can get in and out of places without anyone noticing. It's so secret that it doesn't even have a name, does it?'

'I said, "What helicopter?"' the pilot reiterated in a blank voice.

Lesh looked chastened, but he was still glancing around him at the inside of the machine.

The Squad sat on the two rows of seats that were riveted to the floor on either side of the small fuselage, then fastened their harnesses.

The journey was strange because, even though they covered 200 kilometres in an hour, the helicopter was quiet and they barely felt any motion. It was more like they imagined a spaceship would feel than being thrown around while on a normal military helicopter. Beneath them the hills and fields were black. The chopper had no lights on and inside only a red light shone, meaning that when they reached their destination, their eyes would be accustomed to the dark immediately. Lesh wondered if the helicopter could be seen or heard from the ground at all. He made mental notes about the trip in his head, things he would never be allowed to write down.

Kester sat with his eyes closed, busy running the briefing for the night through his head. Planning what he would do if certain things happened. He glanced at Lily and the others and could see that they were doing the same.

Exactly as planned, the helicopter dropped them on the other side of a hill from the target, so that there was no chance the aircraft would be overheard arriving. It was the perfect way of getting them close in.

The helicopter hovered over an outcrop of rocks surrounded by dense forest as, one by one, the children descended fifty metres via a centimetre-thick wire. They were blown about by the updraught that the helicopter created. Because they were on a mission, their senses were more alive: the noise of the zip wire, the earthy smells coming from the woods, everything was sharp and utterly clear.

Soon they were all on the ground and the helicopter was gone, creating an exaggerated stillness around them.

Using hand signals, Kester ordered that they should move in single file from now on, each watching the luminous strip they had all uncovered on the back of their baseball caps. Kester went third in the line, knowing that the one in charge should be neither at the very front nor the very back.

When they were a kilometre from the target, Lesh, who had been tracking their progress on the SpyPad, tapped Kester twice on the shoulder, the signal they had agreed, and Kester gathered the Squad in a tight circle.

'We're really close to them now,' he whispered, 'so hand signals or whispers. OK?' Everyone nodded.

Kester fitted his night-vision goggles and waited for the others to copy him. The sky had cleared and there was enough starlight for the night vision to work well. Now, instead of the world being various shades of black, everything was green-tinged, small wisps of colour moving in their field of vision. Birds. Animals. Kester could never get used to how effective the goggles were: if the suspected terror group didn't have them, then the Squad would have a massive advantage.

'The place we're looking at is a small quarry,' Kester whispered. He was repeating what Jim had already told them, but part of his role was to keep things clear in everybody's mind. 'The four of you will move in and stand ten metres apart. And watch. If you see anything, speak quietly into the comms system. If there's an emergency, blow into the mic three times in quick succession. That's the call sign. OK?'

The other four nodded.

'Lesh,' Kester murmured, 'show us the images, please.'

Lesh flicked on his SpyPad. It glowed red. Red because that was the only colour of light that would not interfere with their night-vision equipment. They huddled in a small circle to observe. Lesh showed them satellite images of the site they were about to recce, zooming in and out to highlight the areas where they would stand.

The quarry looked like a crater from above, a ring of low cliffs surrounding a wooded area the size of a large back garden.

'The intelligence is that the men arrived at 20:27 hours, just before dark and are settled now,' Lesh reported. 'The drone last passed over about an hour ago at 00:47 hours. There has been no movement in the site since 23:00 hours, according to satellite images.'

'Good,' Kester said. 'Remember, the men we're stalking could be highly trained. They may have dangerous material here. Small arms. IEDs. Anti-personnel traps. Take it one step at a time. OK?'

Four more nods.

'Right. Let's go then.'

Approaching the small quarry was not difficult. The woods were creepy and they could barely see between the trees, but their night-vision equipment showed there was nobody moving around. They took every footstep with great care, moving the last ten metres at a crawl. Kester was afraid and excited at the same time. He knew that the others would be feeling the same.

Soon they were all in position around the top of

the quarry. That's when things stopped being easy.

The five of them froze. The drone intelligence had been wrong. The night-vision equipment had missed something.

The men were not all asleep. They were moving around.

THE ENEMY

'There are at least two,' Hatty's whisper came into Kester's earpiece.

Crouching, Kester looked to his right. Even though the targets were active, he had decided to keep the Squad there to find out everything they could. It was too good an opportunity to miss.

Ten metres to Kester's right, Lesh was taking images of what was happening below. Film and stills. Ten metres to his left, Lily was listening, using a power microphone that could pick up voices from over a hundred metres away.

Quietly gathering evidence, Kester thought, *is what we're supposed to do. Not running about being shot at. We work as a team*, he said to himself. *Stick to our brief and we'll be safe, even if the men are up and about.* And the brief? To find out all they could about the target, then get out of there with no direct contact being made.

Kester glanced over to Adnan and Hatty who were on the far side of the small quarry, observing the men through their night-vision equipment. *We could be out of here in minutes,* he thought. *As long as we all keep still and don't make any stupid mistakes.* That was unlikely because they'd practised this sort of action a hundred times.

In fact, it occurred to him that the worst mistakes would be the ones he made. He was leader and his decisions would determine whether his friends lived or died. He swallowed, more resolved than ever to be a worthy leader.

The Squad monitored the camp. There was the smell of a fire, but no sign of smoke and down among the trees some sort of tarpaulin, probably where the men would sleep.

Kester saw Lily signalling after a minute of listening. A quick wave of her hand, behind her back, so no movement could be detected from below. It also saved her from speaking into her mic, creating unnecessary noise. He crawled slowly over to her, checking everything was still stable by looking at Hatty and Lesh. He got two thumbs up from them. Everything was fine. And quiet. He was careful not to change that as he moved round the quarry to Lily.

'There's something funny about this,' Lily whispered when Kester reached her.

'Go on.'

'The voices. The intelligence says they could be Arabic perhaps?'

Kester nodded.

'I don't think they are. I think it's a European

language. But they're speaking so quietly . . .' Lily hesitated. 'It's hard to work out what it is. This mic is rubbish.'

'OK. We'll report that back to Jim.'

'We might . . .' Lily went on. 'But if I could just get a bit closer . . .'

'No. That's not our brief,' Kester whispered. 'We're meant to observe the site from fifty metres, then report back. That's all.'

Suddenly there was a movement behind Kester. He looked round sharply, wondering who it could be or what, and he was surprised to see Hatty right next to him.

'What?' he whispered harshly. 'You freaked me out. You're supposed to be . . .'

'Let Lily get closer,' Hatty said. 'Just a bit. There's a track that goes down over there. It'd be easy.'

'No,' Kester said. 'Go back.'

'It could be really important,' Hatty argued.

Kester closed his eyes. He was the leader, not Hatty. And, for him, that meant sticking to the brief that Jim had given. But Hatty did have a point. If he could talk to Jim, Jim might say go ahead, let Lily get closer. But Jim wasn't there and it was too dangerous to make radio contact.

It was Kester's call. That was his job: to make calls like this. He looked down into the quarry at the track Hatty had pointed out. *Maybe*, he thought. *So long as we don't take any more risks.*

'I'll go with you,' he said to Lily.

Lily smiled. 'Thanks. Just near enough to hear a bit more.'

But Hatty was shaking her head. 'Not you. You're leader, Kester. If something goes wrong, you're needed up here to oversee. I'll go.'

Kester closed his eyes again. Hatty! Was he really the leader? Who was in charge of this mission? He felt angry with her now, wondering if she was trying to undermine every decision that he made. But he also knew that – this time – she was right.

He sighed.

'OK,' he said evenly. 'Go down halfway. No further. We'll monitor you from up here.'

Kester saw Hatty grin. He refused to grin back at her.

Lily and Hatty located the start of the track and checked each other to make sure that all their visible skin was still covered in cam cream. Then they were off.

Hatty led the way. Her task was to find the right place to observe from and set Lily up to do her listening. They had a tight brief from Kester – go no further than a large fallen tree trunk halfway down the cliff edge – and Hatty knew to stick to it. He had compromised already, showing he could be flexible as a leader and therefore a good one. She would not let him down now.

They moved slowly down the path in the dark,

placing each foot with care, checking the ground for traps and mines and not going so close to the edge that they risked sending stones and loose earth down into the clearing.

Hatty was trying to breathe slow and deep, but she was so excited that she felt she was panting loudly like a dog. She was extremely nervous, but also elated. She loved the way the danger of missions made her feel alive.

On the edge of the quarry, above them, Kester observed the two girls and Adnan.

Lily followed Hatty to the tree trunk where they squatted in absolute silence, listening, trying to hear above the noise of a small waterfall or stream further on. As Lily looked down, she could make out a tent, the embers of a fire and a large metal container. The container looked interesting and she registered it, but she knew she had something more important to concentrate on.

Listening.

The voices she could hear were male.

She held her breath for a few seconds to hear them properly, then nodded to Hatty. She knew exactly what language these men were speaking.

Hatty looked up the hill and put her thumbs up, ready to turn and leave, but then she felt a strong hand pushing her shoulder down. She turned swiftly, ready to fight, just managing to stop herself striking Lily who was the one pushing her.

Hatty ducked with Lily behind the tree trunk, trusting the younger girl's instincts. Footsteps crunched through the ferns and broken twigs.

At first, Hatty feared it was a wolf, stalking them, and was – strangely – relieved to see a man stumbling down the hill.

Had he seen them? Who was he? How had they missed him? Were there more?

Hatty watched him stopping to zip up his fly, then falling back on to the tree trunk and laughing. He was so close that she could smell the sour alcohol coming from him.

He's drunk, she thought. *That's probably good. He's less likely to notice us.*

Neither Lily nor Hatty spoke. They kept every muscle tense to avoid the slightest movement. The next thirty seconds were vital.

Was this man actually going to leave?

And then he belched.

Hatty curled her lip in disgust, then she watched as Lily took a further risk, easing a night-vision camera out of one of the pockets in her cargo pants. If she could just get an image of him, it might help.

Lily lifted the camera slowly, taking care not to raise the lens so high that it might reflect even starlight, then silently snapped a single image, hoping she'd got his face in the frame.

As Lily did all this, Hatty watched her closely. Sometimes Hatty felt that Lily was soft or too nice, a girly girl. And Hatty did not like girly girls. But when they were out in the field like this, she was always reminded – and surprised – that Lily was focused, intelligent and strong-minded. Like now, taking the photo. A great move, a great risk and a great person to be working alongside.

Up above, the three boys had been watching everything. No one moved. No one spoke. They just waited for the man to go. It was clear that he had not seen Lily and Hatty, so everyone knew instinctively, and without discussing it, that the best option was to sit it out and wait, hoping he'd not spot them.

But the moment went on for ages.

Hatty still felt disgust for, rather than fear of, the man.

He's definitely drunk, she thought. *Really drunk. He wouldn't notice if we were sitting here next to a campfire toasting marshmallows.* But all the same, she knew it was the right thing to sit it out.

As they waited for him to move, Lily's mind was burning with her new knowledge. About the voices she'd heard. The men were speaking Russian. Now she was desperate to get this piece of intelligence out of the quarry, through the woods and the darkness and back to Jim. Because she knew it meant everything.

LATE

Jim Sells was standing behind the rest of the footballers when the Squad came down to the hotel breakfast room the next morning. Behind him were a row of counters filled with cereals, meat, fruit and bread, food that the children were finding unusual because there were none of the brands they knew from home. Bright lights illuminated the white tables where the other players sat.

Jim looked furious.

Because Lesh, Lily, Hatty, Kester and Adnan were late. Very late.

They had returned to the hotel at 3.55 a.m. Less than four hours ago. Adnan had said he'd get them all up in time, but had slept through his alarm. Now they were absolutely shattered, as well as flustered because they were late.

'Had a good lie-in?' Jim shouted, making the staff behind the counters stop what they were doing in shock.

'Sorry, Jim,' Adnan said in a quiet voice, hoping to take the flak for the others.

'Sorry isn't good enough, children!' Jim shouted. 'When I say breakfast at seven, I mean breakfast at seven. Breakfast at seven: training at nine. It's our first game today. Remember that? This afternoon?'

'Sorry,' the other four Squad members said, all fully aware that Jim had used the word 'children' to make them feel even smaller.

Kester scanned the rest of the youth team, most of whom were just looking at their plates, not wanting to get involved when someone else was being told off. But three of them were staring back at the Squad, their faces full of glee.

Rio.

Georgia.

Finn.

'We're sorry to the rest of you too,' Kester said, meaning it.

'You might be sorry,' Jim cut in, 'but this is not acceptable. Nor was the brawl between you and Rio. Tomorrow – win, lose or draw today – I want you down here for breakfast at six.'

Lesh saw Rio and Georgia grin, then Finn laugh.

Jim heard the laugh and turned sharply. 'And that's all of you. Not just the ones who were late. All of you will be here for breakfast at six.'

Kester watched the smile drop instantly from Rio's

face, then saw, under the table, his fists clenching and unclenching.

More trouble brewing, Kester thought. He'd had quite enough of that last night.

After they had avoided the belching man and gathered together away from the quarry, it had taken the Squad two hours to get back from the woods, returning the way they'd come.

Back at the hotel, they were desperate to go to sleep, but they gathered dutifully in Kester's room, sitting round the lounge table for a debrief with Jim.

After every mission it was the drill to debrief as soon as was possible, before any mission details were forgotten. They told Jim everything in full detail, leaving nothing out. They showed him the images and films they'd taken, the exact positions of the men, objects they had with them, readings for radioactivity and the presence of explosives.

Jim took the information in, his face calm and his voice unchanged, until he heard the news that the voices were Russian. Then his mood changed.

'Are you sure, Lily?' he asked.

'Yes.'

'Really sure?'

'Yes.'

'Well, that changes everything,' Jim said gravely.

'But there's more,' Lily intervened.

'Go on.'

'I saw a box. It looked like it could contain some sort of weapon.'

Lily watched Jim nod gravely.

'But I didn't see what it was. It was too far off,' Lily went on. 'To get any closer would have jeopardized the overall mission.'

'OK,' Jim said. 'You made the right choice, but did you notice anything about it? Metal? Wood? Any writing on it?'

'Metal, I think,' Lily said, disconsolate. 'Lesh took some images, but they don't show anything worthwhile.'

'Not to worry, Lily.' Jim smiled. 'You've done really well.'

'I did manage to get a photo of the man,' Lily volunteered.

Jim clapped his hands together. 'Now you're talking. Well done, Lily.'

Lily smiled at their commander as she showed him the image. But Jim did not return the smile. His face twitched, then he went pale.

'What is it, Jim?' Kester asked, looking at the image of a man with dark eyes and a screwed up, lined face.

'I need to talk to London,' Jim spluttered.

The five children looked at each other.

'What does that mean?' Hatty demanded.

'Calling London?' Jim asked.

'Yes.'

'It means this mission and the threat to England's security are suddenly a whole lot more serious and dangerous.' He stood up.

'So who's the pretty boy in the photo?' Adnan joked.

'An old friend,' Jim said grimly. 'No. I should say an old enemy. His name is Boris Svidrigaylov. Svid for short.'

'Who is he?' asked Kester.

'There are bad men in this world,' Jim growled. 'Killers. Torturers. Those kinds of people. But there are worse. There are men who would happily encourage wars and conflict and chaos just because they have some twisted grudge against a country or a person. Svidrigaylov is one of those men.'

'And you knew him?' Hatty asked.

'He was around when I was in Moscow. He worked for the KGB, the Russian spy service. But he was too evil for them, so he was kicked out. That was when he started to commit even more appalling acts.'

The children looked at Jim, waiting to hear more, but he was done.

'I need to call London,' he said. 'Bed. All of you. You've done a great thing tonight. Well done.'

They'd finally got to bed at five. All with a firm hand-shake and an enthusiastic thank you from Jim. He was delighted with them.

Which was why the over-the-top telling-off at breakfast was so hard to take.

Jim was pretending to be furious with them so that the others didn't sense that they had a special relationship. 'I'll be harder on you than them,' he had said the day before. Now they knew he meant it.

When the telling-off was over, Lily grabbed toast and jams from the breakfast bar for everyone. Lesh got some fruit. Hatty yoghurts. Kester juices. And Adnan sorted coffees, whether they wanted it or not. It would help to keep them awake. As they gathered their food, they muttered more apologies to the others.

Once Jim – still pretending he was furious – had gone, Rio stood up. He positioned himself behind the rest of the footballers, facing the Squad, making out he represented all their feelings.

'What's going on?' he complained.

Kester knew this was his question to field. He carried on chewing his piece of toast, but looked up to see what mood Rio was in. Was he going to fight or just shout?

Rio was staring straight at Kester, his eyes bulging, losing his cool as he waited for a response. Next to him Georgia had her arms folded across her chest. She looked calmer and, in a way, more dangerous than Rio.

The room was quiet now. The temperature seemed to have dropped several degrees.

'I said, "What's going on?"' Rio repeated.

'We said we're sorry,' Kester said clearly and calmly. 'And we are. It won't happen again.'

'That's not good enough!' Rio shouted, the veins on his neck standing out. 'You were late. Thanks to you we have to be up for six tomorrow.'

'I'm not getting up at six,' Georgia spat.

Kester shrugged. Rio was really losing it, getting angry instead of thinking clearly. Kester could handle him better when he was like this. So long as it didn't turn into another fight.

But then Georgia was speaking in a controlled voice. 'No. There's more to it than that,' she said slowly, like she was just working something out.

Kester sensed the other footballers register what Georgia had said. They'd stopped chewing or were holding their mugs in mid-air. And Kester knew this was it: the challenge. The moment that they knew they would have to deal with when they had to convince everyone they were just normal footballers. The mission depended on it. This was dangerous. Not as immediately dangerous as stalking three Russians in the night woods, but just as threatening to the mission's success.

'We were late,' Kester said, matching Georgia's calm. 'I was meant to get the others up. I slept in. I'm sorry.'

'That's it. That's what worries me,' Georgia said. 'How come you're all so close? You said, when you came here, that you'd never met before. But you're like lifelong mates. Look at just now: you all knew exactly what each of you wanted for breakfast. Things like that are weird.'

Kester looked up. He saw all the other footballers looking quizzically at him now, like they were questioning the Squad and who they really were. He knew he was meant to speak next, to say something that would put all their minds at rest.

But what could he say? Kester needed inspiration.

'It's all part of Jim's master plan,' Lily cut in.

Kester kept his eyes on the footballers. He had to go with what Lily said, whatever it was, so he nodded, pretending to know exactly what she was about to say.

'It's Jim's orders,' Lily explained. 'Forward players, like most of you, are team members, but you also have individual flair.' She paused, hoping they'd like that. 'But defenders have to work together. We're not individuals. We're one line of defence.' Lily was getting into her stride now. 'Our strength is in how we work as a unit. How we can rely on each other. That's why we got each other's breakfast. As a team. That's why we rely on each other to wake up. Jim did this sort of thing with Real Madrid. You're right to say that we've not known each other long. We haven't. So we're doing everything we can to compensate for that.'

Kester wanted to laugh. Lily was a genius. What

an answer! He saw most of the footballers nodding. All except Rio and Georgia.

'Well, you're not doing a very good job of it,' Rio said, scowling.

'Come on.' A voice from the doorway. Jim. 'Time to get on to the training fields. Just a gentle hour session this morning. We've a game in seven hours. Train. Rest. Eat. Then on the bus to the stadium. OK?'

Everyone was on their feet and walking to the exit, excited now the game was only a few hours away, forgetting the argument and the secrets Rio and Georgia had been close to uncovering.

But Kester noticed that Rio was hanging back, wanting to be the last to leave the room. So Kester stayed back too. He needed to know what Rio had to say.

'I suppose we're about to see how good a defence you are now then, aren't we?' Rio sneered.

'That's right,' replied Kester, trying to sound as confident as he could. But he didn't like the look on Rio's face at all. Rio was not satisfied by what he'd heard. He was a boy who wanted answers.

ENGLAND V FAROE ISLANDS

What with training and the mission, there had not been much time for the five Squad members to think about representing their country at football.

But now the full realization of what was happening hit them: they were walking in a line of footballers kitted out in white opposite another team wearing blue, coming out from under the stand on to the massive green football pitch of Wisła's stadium. For the Squad this was their second visit to the Wisła Stadium, but it was different in that there was a crowd of 500 people watching in the main stand, their applause bouncing around to create the unusual atmosphere of a stadium neither full nor empty.

Hatty and the others felt excited, anxious and confused, but that was normal for them. Every mission they went out on was dangerous. They could be exposed at any time or they could be shot at. Part of their job was to mask their fears and carry on doing what they needed to do. This was just the same. No one would actually die out there on the football pitch, but if they went out of the competition, and therefore had to leave the country, the England team could die. They'd faced stakes just as high when they had gone into the Ukrainian woods the night before.

Jim gathered the team in a circle before kick-off.

'This is not going to be easy,' he said. 'You might think the Faroe Islands are a weak country, but their players know each other. They've trained and played together much more than we have.'

'That's true,' Rio snorted.

'What was that, Rio?' Jim asked sharply.

'Nothing.'

'OK,' Jim continued. 'So I want you to play to your strengths. Forwards, attack. You have the flair and the skill. Defenders, get the ball to the forwards quickly. Don't pass it to and fro. Keep it simple.'

Everyone nodded.

'And remember,' Jim finished. 'This is a game we have to win. Lose and we go straight home.'

Once Jim was off the pitch, Rio kept them in their circle and started talking. 'I don't know about all of you, but I want to meet the England team. Jim said we'd meet the players if we get to the final, so that's exactly what's going to happen. Do we all understand?'

Several of the players said 'yes', including Squad members, even though what Rio was saying sounded like a threat.

Then Georgia, fixing her hair behind an Alice

band, spoke. 'If I don't get to meet the players, there will be serious trouble. It's a big opportunity for me.'

Hatty shook her head, catching Lily's eye. Lily was stifling a laugh. They both knew what Georgia was thinking: that she was going to meet one of the younger players and he was going to fall in love with her, marry her and she'd be the next Victoria Beckham or Cheryl Cole.

Hatty did absolutely nothing to hide her smirk.

The game started well. Lesh was half-pleased and half-dismayed to note that Rio was a superb footballer and was completely dominating the midfield while doing a lot to protect the defence. He was also brilliant at creating goals.

After three minutes, Rio drew two defenders towards him and slotted a ball through for Hatty to run on to and score England's first goal; she received a hug or a pat from every one of the team except Georgia.

Twenty-nine minutes in, Rio put a free kick perfectly on to Johnny's head for him to grab England's second goal.

And ten minutes after half-time, Rio ran the ball solo through four tackles, then chipped it over the keeper. England's third. Rio was the captain, the best player and the source of everything good about the team going forward.

The problems were at the back.

Like the young Wisła players the day before, it didn't take long for the Faroe Islands team to expose the England defence. A couple of short passes were enough to open up huge gaps between Hatty, Lesh, Lily and Kester's backline.

In the first hour the Faroes had run the ball through the England defence a dozen times, to find themselves clear on goal. Five of those times they'd missed the target. Three of those times Adnan had made superb saves. But four of those times they'd scored.

So, with only a few minutes left, it was England 3 Faroe Islands 4.

Rio was going mental. 'What the hell are you doing?' he shouted at the defenders. 'Every time it's the same. Track the players. Don't lunge in and tackle. Wait. They're making monkeys out of you.'

Hatty watched Rio getting more and more cross. She understood what was at stake for him. Football was his life and that was reflected in his attitude.

With three minutes left, Rio was playing deeper and deeper, trying to stop the defence conceding again. But that was not going to do them any good at all and Hatty knew it. His actions were causing the whole England team to play that way, making them focus on defence, not attack. Their weakness, not their strength.

Hatty realized she had to do something radical, so she snapped.

'Go upfield!' she shouted at Rio. 'We need a goal. You're the only way we're going to get one.'

'While you lot let another one in?' Rio yelled back. 'How can I?'

'So what if we let one more in? We need to take a risk. We're better at attacking than defending, therefore we should attack. If we don't score in the next three minutes, we're out anyway.'

With that, Rio paused. Hatty was right. But would he admit it? She waited for a response from her team captain.

'OK,' Rio spluttered. 'But I'm going to go mad after this! It's a joke you lot playing for England.'

'Fine,' she agreed. 'Go mad. But let's get out of this hole first.'

And, to her surprise, Rio did what she said. He went to stand on the halfway line.

Hatty made sure the next time the Faroes came forward that she won the ball. She gave it everything, took possession and fired a long hard pass upfield.

To Rio.

Hatty watched Rio control it, take it past two defenders, advance on goal, wait for the keeper to commit himself, then hammer the ball to his left. It flew hard and straight, a few centimetres off the ground all the way into the back of the net.

4–4.

The England players mobbed their captain.

Everyone off the pitch was looking at him, cheering. He'd saved them.

Hatty caught the eye of Jim on the touchline. But he wasn't looking at Rio, like everyone else. He was looking at Hatty and he was clapping her.

A 1–4 final score meant a penalty shoot-out. Five shots each. The team that scored the most would win.

Adnan saved every shot aimed at his goal. Three out of three. Leaping to his left, leaping to his right and tipping the third over the bar. And that was enough because England had converted their first three. The shoot-out ended 3–0.

It was over. England had won.

At the end Rio jogged over to Hatty and Adnan, who were standing together. Hatty was not sure what to expect, so she was surprised when Rio shook Adnan's hand.

'Well played. You're a good keeper,' Rio said to him as Kester caught up with them and clapped Adnan on the back.

'Brilliant, mate,' Kester said.

Then Rio stopped in front of all of them, glaring at Kester. 'But just because he saved three penalties, don't think that I'm not going to go crazy in there. The argument is only just beginning. I want you five off the team.'

KESTER'S CHALLENGE

Kester drew back from the players as they funnelled towards the tunnel under the main stand. He wanted to be sure to shake every Faroe Island player's hand, having noticed that Rio, the so-called captain, hadn't. He knew it was important to show respect to the opposition, whoever they were and whatever the score.

He had another reason to hold back too. If Jim wanted to talk to him, this would be the only opportunity before they were with everyone else in the dressing room, before the inevitable post-match squabble.

'How are we going to play this?' Kester asked Jim when they were alone.

Jim smiled. 'It won't be easy, Kester. That was a close game. If Rio starts saying our defence is shaky, he'll have a point.'

'He's a big problem,' said Kester.

'He is,' Jim nodded, 'but spying is a problem, a series of problems that we have to overcome. Look:

you were in danger when you monitored the target last night. But you improvised and came back with more information than we imagined you would. If anything, this new situation is more dangerous. If we don't get you close to that group of men in the next few days, we'll have nothing. The whole mission will be washed up. We need to get out there again tonight . . .'

'Tonight?' Kester was shocked.

'Yes. Tonight.'

'The others are shattered, Jim.'

'Well, we'd best go and get Rio sorted, so you can all go and have a sleep then,' Jim continued. 'We need intelligence, like what's inside the metal container that Lily saw and what they are planning to do with it. If we can find that out, then we'll be so much closer to knowing what Svid is planning and how we can stop it. The hardware they have will determine what they're going to do – and how.'

'But why would Svid want to do anything like this?' Kester asked. 'I still don't get it.'

'A number of reasons. But the main one is that he hates the Russian government because they are England's allies now, sort of, so he wants to undermine Russia's relationships with other countries. And this would be perfect. Imagine a Russian murdering the whole of the England team. Diplomatic relations would never survive that. Svid liked it best when no one trusted anyone else, when the Russians spent a lot of money on spies and defence. If that all comes back, he'll be rich and powerful again. That's his motivation.'

'Sounds like a headcase,' Kester offered.

'He is that,' Jim smiled. 'Look. I suspect our team will be going out in the next round, so then we'll all be on our way home. That makes tonight all the more important.'

'OK,' Kester said. 'That's fine. Who have we got in the next round anyway?'

Jim grinned.

'Who?' Kester pressed.

'Spain,' Jim replied, deadpan. 'The favourites.'

Kester put his hand to his head. 'Oh no . . .'

Jim and Kester could hear shouting as they approached the England dressing room, but as soon as Jim entered the room, the noise stopped.

'OK,' said Jim. 'What's going on?'

Rio stood, red in the face and surrounded by discarded boots, shin pads and towels.

'Yes, Rio?' Jim pressed.

'I don't understand,' Rio stated in a quiet voice.

Kester almost smiled. This was good from Rio. He was showing uncharacteristic control.

'You don't understand what, Rio?' Jim asked, still calm.

Rio edged forward across the tiles towards a massage table that stood in the centre of the room.

'This new defence, with respect, Jim, is not good enough. We're representing England here. And, apart from Adnan at the end, I've seen nothing to suggest these are quality players.'

'Give it time, Rio,' Jim countered. 'You've not played together before. And we improved as a team as the game progressed.'

'With respect again, Jim, we were playing the weakest footballing nation in Europe. I take it Spain beat Poland?'

'They did, Rio.'

'So we have to play Spain next. If anything, Spanish youth players are better than the adults. They'll pass the ball through us like a knife through butter.'

Jim nodded. 'Like I said, Rio, we're improving as a team. We'll do more defensive work. It'll be OK.'

'Not against Spain,' Rio argued. 'They'll crush us.'

'We have the players we have, Rio,' Jim said, his voice rougher now. 'I'm the coach and I'm going to get you through this. You're the captain, Rio, and a good one. Let's try to sound like we're on the same side, yes?'

Rio shook his head, but said nothing: Jim had argued him down. But now Georgia was on her feet.

'They're not good enough to defend for England,' Georgia stated, glancing at the Squad, who were sitting with their backs to a tiled wall.

'Like I said,' Jim repeated, 'they're improving.'

'But they're not good defenders,' Georgia went on. 'They don't know how to do it. They're not fit to wear the shirt.'

Jim was cross now, but there was not much else he could say. He was in an impossible position. The Squad were weak defenders. They weren't fit to wear the shirt. Not this shirt. If only he could explain to the rest of the team that the new defenders had been brought in to protect the England men's team, then he felt sure that even Rio and Georgia would understand. But the mission was a secret and it had to stay that way.

And because Jim had no answer that would satisfy Georgia or Rio, there was still too much doubt about the Squad, meaning the success of the mission was in the balance. Kester knew that it was now or never. He had one card that he thought he could play. Something that Georgia had said. It might work. It might not. But he had to give it a go.

'Rio?' he said, standing to face the captain.

'Uh-huh.'

'Do you agree with that?'

'What?'

'That if we can't defend, we shouldn't be allowed to play. That if someone doesn't do their job, they shouldn't be allowed to do it again.'

Rio nodded.

'So what is a captain supposed to do?' Kester asked.

'Captain,' Rio replied with a grin.

'What does that mean?'

'Boss the team on the pitch.'

'And . . .'

'Er . . .' Rio looked puzzled for a moment before answering. 'Represent the team off it.'

'So why did you storm off the pitch after the game and not shake hands with any of the Faroes players?' Kester held up the Faroe Island shirt he had just swapped for his England top. 'We've just scraped past a minnow. They nearly had the result of their lives against a massive footballing country – England. The home of football. And the England captain didn't even shake their hands at the end.'

Rio looked embarrassed. He had no answer to that.

'So do you accept that if we failed as defenders, then you failed as captain?' Kester concluded his argument. Rio didn't respond. He just looked furious.

There was silence in the room. A silence that none of the players or Jim seemed ready to fill. Kester understood that he could take control now, he could fill the silence.

'How about a challenge?' he said.

The rest of the Squad looked at Kester, puzzled.

'How about you try to captain five of your attackers against my four defenders and Adnan in goal? Attack against defence. Then we'll see who lives up to their title. Good captain or good defender?'

Rio was grinning. 'Bring it on,' he said. 'It's going to be a walkover.'

Kester looked at the Squad members' faces as Rio spoke. All four were open-mouthed and horrified. But Kester hoped that, rather than having put them in an impossible and humiliating position, he had just in fact saved the day and deflected the heat from Jim and their mission tonight.

PLAIN SAILING

The Squad met Jim in Adnan's room after the rest of the players had gone to bed. Jim needed to brief them about the night's mission: the helicopter was picking them up in two hours at the same spot as the night before.

'Right,' Jim said, 'we know where the target has settled for the night. They've crossed the border into Poland, as we expected. We have images from the drone and satellite.'

'Where are they?' Kester asked.

'About two hundred kilometres away in a steep valley with a meandering river at the bottom,' Jim said. 'There's a single track to the building they're staying in. It's a mountain refuge in a canyon: just a wooden hut really. There are lots of huts like that scattered through the mountains.'

'And they're guarding the track,' Hatty added. 'So we can't go along that.'

'They appear to have set tripwires on the track, yes. But that does create an opportunity.' Jim's voice was slightly uneven as he spoke and the five children knew they were about to hear why they were not going to have an easy night.

The helicopter took the Squad swiftly across the mountains and forests of the far south-east of Poland, covering part of the same terrain as it had the night before. It dropped them in a remote part of the Bieszczady National Park, by a wide river, with no towns or villages for kilometres. Just like the night before, they had all changed into black clothing and smeared their faces with cam cream.

Soon the five children were standing by a wide, shallow river under a dark but star-scattered sky. According to Jim's briefing, the last part of their journey would be made by raft.

They found the raft easily. Six medium-sized trunks bound to each other by twisted rope.

'Is that thing safe?' Hatty asked. 'I mean we arrive on a secret twenty-first-century helicopter to find that the next stage of our journey is on a pile of logs.'

Now everyone was looking at Adnan who knelt to study the raft, testing the tension of the rope and feeling the wood to make sure it was sound. Eventually he turned to Kester.

'You're in charge now, Adnan,' Kester said. 'Anything on the river is your call.'

Adnan nodded, a serious look on his face. 'The

raft is sound,' he said. Then he picked up a long wooden pole. 'The pole is to steer it with and it's only effective if a river is calm. And the intelligence said it was calm all the way, didn't it, Lesh?'

Lesh consulted his SpyPad. 'Yes. All the way down to the target and beyond. It should be flat with no rapids. We're just going to be drifting.'

'Good,' Adnan said. 'Look, we trained for this in England. It was pretty rough there too. This is going to be like punting in Cambridge compared to that. It'll be fun. Let's get on board.'

'Fun?' Lesh muttered. 'There's an armed gang of psychos at the other end.'

They launched the raft by pushing it into the shallows and quickly distributing their weight. Hatty stayed in the water at first, to guide the raft away from the bank, up to her hips in the river before she scrambled aboard.

'Cold?' Adnan asked her.

'Just a bit,' Hatty said with a false smile.

Adnan took the wooden pole and began to use it to guide the raft along the river in the dark. Lesh and Lily sat at the front, night-vision goggles on, directing him away from outcrops of rock. There were not many obstacles though, and the water was slow and easy to navigate.

Lesh sat with the SpyPad hidden under his jacket, so that its light didn't show, having linked it to a satellite above. He monitored where they were, a red dot flickering on the map of the river as they made their way. When he looked up, he saw Adnan smiling.

'Why are you grinning, Adnan?'

'Good memories actually,' Adnan replied.

No one responded: they knew he was thinking about his parents in a happy way. He often talked about how they had taken him rafting. The others knew to let him enjoy it. Most of the time their memories were bad.

The Squad had three hours to complete their mission.

First, take the raft seven kilometres downriver to the target.

Second, observe the target and check out what materials the men had with them.

Third, get back on the raft and navigate it to a helicopter pick-up point another eight kilometres downriver.

All without being seen.

The rafting along the river was, as Adnan had said, easy. No rapids. No dangerous bends. No sudden drop in the water level. They moved swiftly without any worries, until they neared their target, the river moving faster as they got closer. Now they were near, they started tensing up: there was less talking, tighter body language and invisible signals passing between them to say that it was nearly time to get to work.

For the last kilometre they travelled in silence.

Adnan kept the raft in the deeper, smoother water, to avoid making noises that might give them away.

In their minds they were all rehearsing their role in the mission.

Kester, Lesh and Hatty had to climb the gorge's side and direct – using the night-vision equipment and radios – what Lily and Adnan would do below.

Lily and Adnan needed to get close to the hut, locate the container that Lily had seen the night before and work out what was in it. Was it military hardware? And if so, what?

Lily also had to listen in to gather any more intelligence and, if possible, put tracking devices on rucksacks and the large metal box.

That was it.

Then they had to get out of there.

When the raft reached the place they needed to disembark, the Squad climbed off one by one, as Adnan held it steady.

They were at the bottom of a dark canyon. It was a black enough night, but without light from the moon, it was dismal. They all fitted their night-vision goggles to help them see, but it remained murky. Tree branches and other plants dangled around them, dripping water on their faces. There was no sound of animals or birds. They could smell the rotting vegetation in the still air.

'OK,' Kester whispered, their heads all close together. 'We all know what we have to do. Just remember we're up against men that Jim rates as among the most dangerous in the world. They won't be expecting us, but they'll be brutal if they catch us.'

Everyone nodded, then they were off.

Kester, Hatty and Lesh scrambled up a steep hillside to where they needed to be within ten minutes, moving round the back of the target to stay concealed. They had to negotiate rocks and scree, but it wasn't too difficult. When they emerged above and behind the mountain hut, there was no sign of the men, just a night-vision green scene below. So green it was like they were at the bottom of the sea.

When Lesh saw a flicker of light coming from inside the wooden shack, he nudged Kester. The men must be inside. There were no other bodies visible.

'All clear,' Kester whispered into his mic and he settled down to monitor Lily and Adnan.

Because they were higher than the river now, they could hear its sounds. It was noisy, water being thrown wildly against rocks and forced through channels.

'I thought the river was meant to be calm,' Hatty whispered. 'For us to get away.'

Kester nodded. 'It does sound like rapids.'

'How are we going to get the raft down rapids when we're done?' Lesh asked.

Then Lily's voice came over the radio. 'Going in.'

This was exactly as they'd planned. The three above would direct the two below.

'Move north-east-east, keeping low,' Kester whispered.

They could see Lily and Adnan crawling in the dark towards the wooden shack.

'Let's worry about our exit strategy later,' Kester whispered. 'We need to get Lily and Adnan in and out. Everything else is secondary to that.'

Hatty nudged Kester. 'What?' he whispered, worried one of the men was coming out.

'There,' Hatty said. 'Against the shack. The box.'

Kester looked and grinned, then radioed Lily and Adnan. 'To the right of the shack. Possible box.'

'Roger,' Lily said.

Kester and the others watched Lily change direction and move to the right of the shack. Adnan stayed where he was, observing its doorway from behind two trees.

It wasn't long before Kester saw a glow coming from the side of the shack: Lily, on her knees, shining a red filter torch on to the box. Gathering evidence.

'Bingo,' she whispered. 'There's writing on it. Serbo-Croat, I think. I'm taking photos.'

Kester felt good. This was going well. Then he saw two things that made his heart miss a beat. First, Adnan ducking behind the trees, whispering 'Conceal.' Second, Lily tucking her legs in and rolling away from the shack door.

'What is it?' Kester radioed, but knew he wouldn't get an answer.

He heard a muffled male voice, then saw another red glow flare up then die down. A cigarette being lit. Someone was outside. No one had heard the door opening. But there was more noise coming from up by the river.

'Stay down,' Kester whispered to Lily. He could feel his stomach twisting. Here he was again, responsible for one of his friends. He needed to make the right decisions and he thought keeping their heads down was the best plan.

All five children held their breath as the man breathed smoke out into the night. Hatty slipped her night goggles off. The starlight was not enough for the man to be able to see anything with his bare eyes.

'He won't be able to see you,' Hatty whispered through the radio. 'He's just come out of a well-lit hut.'

Again there was no reply.

Lily lay still, barely breathing, the man's feet within centimetres of her legs. She knew to be calm, not to panic. If she moved, he would find her and that would be it. Who knew what would happen? Lily tried not to think about it as she lay, watching his feet tapping on the floor, not enjoying the acrid smell of his tobacco.

It's going to be OK, she told herself. *He'll finish his cigarette and then go back inside.* That's what Lily hoped.

When the man did finish, he dropped his cigarette on Lily's hand. She muffled a cry into her jacket as the cigarette burned into her skin.

For a second the man stopped moving into the hut. From above Hatty could see that he was looking around, wondering if he had heard an animal. But then he carried on inside, rubbing his hands together.

When he was gone, Lily knocked the cigarette end away and tried to breathe more deeply, feeling her body relax. She flicked on her red torch again. Her hand was very painful – the cigarette had burned deep into her flesh – but she dismissed it. She had a job to do.

The box was as long and wide as Lily. Whatever was inside it, it would be big enough to contain her. She shuddered at the thought as she took photographs of the side of the box, mostly words in Serbo-Croat and a string of numbers. One thing she did guess was that the box had some sort of military hardware in it, and she thought to open it, but could see that it was padlocked. There was no way she could get into it without creating a noise that would give her away.

Now she had to get back to Jim so they could work out what Svid was carrying. But before she left, she slipped a tracking pin out of her cargo pants and stuck it on the underside of the container. Now they would know exactly where the container was 24/7. Lily felt a little more secure now and could at least give in to her pain. She crept slowly away from the hut towards Adnan and gestured to the others that they should come down off the hill. It was time to leave.

*

Fifteen minutes later, all five were back beside the river, ready to launch the raft. Lily was dipping her hand into the cold water of the river.

'How's your hand?' Kester asked.

'Fine.'

'Is it?' Hatty wasn't so sure.

'No, but we've got more to worry about than one of us having a minor injury,' Lily said. 'Let's get out of here.'

'Adnan?' Kester said. 'We need your expertise here. It looks like the intelligence was wrong. There may be rapids ahead. It's not going to be easy. Can we escape on the raft?'

'It's a huge risk,' Adnan confessed.

Then Lesh was pointing. Back the way they'd come. Two torchlight beams were suddenly visible, coming down the hill towards them.

'There's no time to do a risk assessment,' Hatty spat. 'We need to go. Now.'

'She's right. It's the men,' Kester said, fixing his night goggles on them. 'We need to launch the raft. Rapids or no rapids. Agreed, Adnan?'

'Agreed,' Adnan said, but none of them saw the frown on his face. He knew this was their best option, but it was still a deadly one.

RAPIDS

The raft was exactly where they had left it, secured to some trees and bobbing about in the water like it was keen to get going itself.

The Squad needed to be on it immediately; there was no time to debate whether it was safe or not. Two men were patrolling the area and they could not afford to get caught by them. They climbed on one by one, making sure the raft stayed steady in the water.

As soon as Adnan released the ropes, the raft began to drift down the river. Adnan was deep in thought as he watched the black cavernous rock walls pass by. Normally they were trained to do something over and over again, to iron out any possible mistakes. But last week, back in England, they'd only spent a day river-rafting and it hadn't been too rough. He could tell from his previous experience, by the sound of the river ahead and by the way the land was steep and twisting, that this was going to be severe.

First, he let the raft drift in silence, not yet using

the pole to steer, in case it made too much noise splashing in the water or hitting the rocks. Then the river swung to the left through a steep gorge, still moving slowly.

After a few minutes – and maybe a kilometre's distance – Adnan could feel the raft being pulled faster.

He'd known this was coming and said, 'When it gets rough, keep your body low and hold on to the trunks or the binding rope. Get a really good grip. If you're thrown off, try to steer yourself with the water, rather than swim against it.'

But nobody replied because the raft had suddenly picked up even more speed. Dramatically, almost knocking Adnan into the water.

'What can you see?' he asked Lesh, who was at the front of the raft, his night-vision goggles on.

'Narrow gorge,' Lesh reported. 'The water . . .'

'Yes?'

'The water's churning. There are rocks . . . I think . . .'

Adnan felt like shouting the next instruction, but he wanted the others to remain calm, so he tried to pretend he was too.

'Lie flat. Jam your hands down in the gaps between the logs. Now. And your feet too . . . If you go under . . . just roll with it . . . Don't try to swim up until you know where up is . . .'

The boat was being tossed about now, rocking

violently from side to side, so it was impossible even to speak. The five children held on, heads down, as they saw, in the limited light, the sides of the gorge. It was barely twice as wide as the raft.

'Keep your feet and hands away from the edges . . .'

As Adnan was telling them what to do, the raft hit one side of the canyon hard. He held on, hoping the others were doing what he'd said. If not, they'd be thrown off the raft and tossed into the churning water and in the water it was highly likely they'd be smashed against a rock and killed. Or simply dragged into the cold depths and drowned.

Then the raft seemed to be pitched into the air, and they were drenched in a torrent of water before it landed. Adnan glanced up to see if everyone was still aboard, but before he could look around fully, they hit the side of the canyon again and were submerged in another massive wave of freezing water. They were soaked and cold and out of control.

But now the river wasn't just making them cold and wet, they were finding it hard to breathe, not knowing when they were about to be engulfed by water. Adnan heard coughing and choking and was glad of it: that meant someone was still on the raft with him.

Eventually everything was moving so much faster – and spinning – that Adnan could only concentrate on himself. Hold on. That was all his mind would let him do. All concern for his friends had gone.

There was water everywhere, powerful forces coming from above and below, terrible noise, a roaring so loud that he wasn't sure if he was on top of the raft or underneath it.

Just as Adnan was getting back control of his mind, he was ripped from the raft and turned, water filling his mouth and nose, over and over, round and round. He was cold, so impossibly cold. Adnan gave in to the water, waiting until it calmed, hoping it would calm, so he could conserve his strength for a time when he could use it. He knew he wasn't breathing now, that he must have taken in a huge amount of water, but he was too disoriented to know what to do.

And then the strangest thing happened: his mum and dad came into his head. The day they were shot. Every day for two years he had grieved for them, felt alone, felt that they were far away and gone, but now it was like they were there, their hands reaching out to him, and he wanted to reach out too, to be with them again, not alone in the dark. Mum and Dad.

Suddenly another force took Adnan and he realized that he was no longer churning round and round. He was being pulled up. It was lighter. And he could breathe.

He was out of the river.

The first thing he did was vomit all the water that he had swallowed and breathed in. Then – slowly, painfully – he opened his eyes. He was on his knees.

To his left, Kester's face, pale with bloodshot eyes. To his right, Hatty grinning.

'Nice job, Mr Raft Expert,' Hatty said. 'You were the only one who fell off. We're safe now. All of us. Look.'

Adnan stared hard into Hatty's face and he thought he saw something. A welling of water in the corner of her eye. Then he looked at the others sitting on the raft. They had passed through a very narrow gorge, concealed from above by a tall forest. The river here was calm. He was out of the deep water.

'You've got some water in your eye,' he said to Hatty.

Hatty wiped it away. 'You've got more in yours.'

DEFENDERS

The Squad arrived back at the hotel from the canyon mission at 5 a.m.

On the helicopter journey back across south-east Poland, they'd had no time to go over the mission. Instead, they huddled together and planned the next day's football – the attack and defence idea that Kester had come up with – and how they were going to play it. Their adrenalin was up after the action of the night, but, as it dissipated, they started to feel exhausted, heads aching with the strain of the last few hours and days.

This was a tough week on the Squad physically and mentally – and they were not even halfway through it.

Back at the hotel, Jim gave them a very short debriefing. Lily showed him photographs of the military box she had seen outside the refuge, especially the wording on the side. But not before Jim had personally treated Lily's cigarette burn and then bandaged it.

'I'm pretty sure that it's Serbo-Croat,' Lily said, ignoring the pain in her hand. 'I need to translate it.'

Jim shook his head. 'There's no need.'

'You know what it means?' Hatty asked.

'I know what's in the box,' Jim explained. 'It's a rocket launcher. From the war in Bosnia several years ago. It can pierce tanks and walls at a range of four hundred metres. We have to get it off them.'

There was a moment of silence.

'What would they use it for?' Adnan asked.

'To attack the England team's hotel?' Lily suggested. ·

'Maybe,' said Jim. 'They were used on buildings, vehicles, market places, even at a football stadium once.'

'Why don't we just send an Apache helicopter in and blow them up?' Adnan asked. 'That's what they want to do, so let's go out and blast them first.'

Jim smiled. It was the first time he'd smiled that night. 'I sincerely wish we could, Adnan. But it's more sensitive than that. If we attack someone in Poland, the Poles will go mad. In addition, if we kill Russians in Poland, the Russians will go mad and might claim that the men involved were just studying nature or something like that. We have to do this carefully and sensitively, otherwise we create even more problems than we had in the first place.'

'Hmmmm,' said Adnan.

'Why not tell the Polish authorities as it's on their land?' Hatty added.

'We don't . . . we don't trust anyone at the moment,' Jim stuttered. 'If we can deal with this alone, it will prevent any problems between ourselves and other countries.'

'It's a dangerous tactic,' said Kester. 'Sometime in the next few days these men are going to attack a building or something like that. Loads of people could be killed.'

'It is,' Jim agreed. 'But it's a tactic that's coming from the top, so we stick with it.'

Kester frowned.

'Look, if we need to make a decision to do something and there's no time to contact those in charge, then that's a different matter.' Jim paused, then said, 'Lily? Did you . . .'

'. . . put a tracking device on the container?' Lily replied. 'Yes. And it's not moved since. Lesh has been monitoring it on his SpyPad.'

Jim nodded. 'Good work. Good work, all of you.'

The game of attack and defence between Rio and Kester's teams did not start well, with Georgia smacking the ball against the post within seconds. The Squad had twenty-nine minutes more of relentless attacking to withstand. Five players against five and Jim as the referee.

A minute after Georgia hit the post, Johnny picked

the ball up on the centre line and ran at an angle across Lesh and Lily. As Lesh went in to tackle, Johnny turned and laid the ball back to Rio, who flipped it into the penalty area. Both central defenders were out of the game. And there was Finn, drawing his foot back.

Off his line, Adnan hesitated. Everything seemed to stand still. If Finn chipped him now, it would be an easy goal. But not everything was standing still. Hatty was moving. Coming fast and hard, she clattered the ball away from Finn, conceding a corner.

In fact, it was Hatty who was at the centre of everything now. And Kester, who was meant to be captain, let her get on with it. She seemed to have a natural ability to make the defence work as one. The opposing team came in wave after wave. But tackle after tackle, block after block and save after save kept them out.

Then the forwards changed their tactics. They were keeping the ball further away from the goal, taking long shots instead of trying to pass the ball into the net. It meant that the Squad had to come out to try to block the shots, which also meant that there was space behind the defence.

And suddenly Johnny was in that space, one-on-one with Adnan with ten minutes to go. He seemed certain to score. Lily was behind him with no way of getting the ball. She didn't want to foul him. She thought kicking someone to make them fall over just because she couldn't get to the ball was wrong. But what else could she do? If she didn't trip him, then he'd score. There was no doubt about that.

She made sure it was a gentle foul. Even before Johnny went down, Rio was standing over Lily, his eyeballs popping out of his head.

'Professional foul. You cheating . . . Ref? Ref? Off. She's got to go.'

Jim walked over and put out his hand to Lily who took it to haul herself up. Once she was standing, Jim showed her a red card. Then he winked.

Lily frowned. She felt ashamed at first because she'd never been sent off before, but what she had done had been right. Suddenly the throbbing pain in her hand returned. But, again, she dismissed it.

'Sorry, Johnny,' she said sheepishly, helping him up.

Johnny smiled. 'Don't be. I'd have done the same thing.'

With one minute to go, the forwards had still not scored. Ever since the sending off, Rio had been shouting at his teammates.

'Rattled.' Hatty grinned to Lesh.

Adnan nodded. 'He sure is.'

Rio had given up on teamwork now. He was getting hold of the ball and desperately running at the defenders.

With thirty seconds to go, Finn had the ball, but looked utterly clueless, so Rio whipped it off his feet and started a final fierce run, taking it past Kester, then Hatty, with only Lesh and the keeper to beat.

Lesh lunged at him, thinking he'd got to the ball, but looked up to see Rio one-on-one with Adnan, drawing his foot back to shoot.

Would Adnan be able to save one last shot? Would he be able to prove the defenders were good and put Rio in his place?

The answer was no. The ball was in the back of the net: 1–0 to the attacking side. The Squad were beaten.

'You were outstanding,' Jim said, once he'd gathered the Squad in Kester's hotel room.

'Thanks,' they all said together. Even though they'd lost, they felt like they'd won.

'But now you need some sleep,' Jim went on.

'Sleep?'

'Your next mission is harder and longer than the previous ones. And you've got the Spain game tomorrow. I want you to sleep. Eat anything you want from room service. Rest. This time tomorrow we'll have a briefing about the mission. Then we'll be off to play Spain.'

'What's the mission?' Kester asked, standing. 'Why is it so much harder? I thought you just wanted us to keep watching them and try to find out more about the hardware they have.'

'Because of what you've discovered,' Jim replied,

'there's been a change of plan. But I'll tell you more about it later. Just rest now. I want your minds clear for twenty-four hours.'

BLACK OP

After breakfast, Jim ran a light training session for the whole team in preparation for the Spain game later in the day, then he announced that he was taking the defenders for more intensive training.

'They need it!' Rio shouted after them. Jim, for once, did not respond.

Hatty smiled to herself. If only Rio knew what was really happening, that this intensive training they were going on was not about football at all, but about guns and bombs and protecting his precious England superstars. She burned with the desire to tell him. But of course, she never could.

The Squad gathered on the perimeter of the hotel grounds, all eyes on Jim.

'You want to know what the mission is?' he asked.

'Yes, please,' Hatty answered.

'OK.' Jim cleared his throat. 'The England first team arrive in Krakow tomorrow.'

'Fantastic,' Lily said, grinning at Kester. 'If we could just beat Spain . . .'

Kester grinned back.

'. . . you could meet them,' Jim said, finishing the sentence. 'And I will definitely be using that as motivation with the rest of the team. But back to business. England are in Krakow to train. It's their base. But they will not be playing here. We believe that the men you've been monitoring will attack during England's training camp in this area and not during the tournament. That means any attack will be in the next three days. So . . . we . . . we want you to go in and hit the terrorists and –'

'Hit?' It was Lily who had interrupted.

And for a moment Jim looked surprised. 'Go on, Lily,' he said, regaining his composure.

'Well,' Lily said. 'All we've ever done is monitor, find things out. We do it because we're children and no one suspects us. But this? By "hit" you mean attack, don't you? That's for the Special Forces, isn't it? Not us.'

Jim nodded. 'Normally I would agree too,' he said. 'This is a dangerous assignment. But frankly . . .'

'Yes?' said Hatty.

'Well, frankly you five are the best qualified. You know the terrain. And we can't go about it in the way the Special Forces would anyway. We're watching, tracking, following. And you've done all that superbly so far. The only extra bit is stopping them. Also, if anyone with an interest has any inkling that we're on to them, then we're creating a greater threat. They could well be watching our MI6 and SAS units at home and abroad. But you're here and we need to hit them tonight. They've been moving about a hundred kilometres a day. At that rate they'll reach Krakow late tomorrow. We're assuming that means they could attack any time thirty-six hours from now.'

'But how do we stop them without killing them – or making a scene?' Kester asked.

'Good question, Kester,' said Jim. 'We'll arm you with two kinds of grenade: gas grenades and stun grenades, the first to knock people out, the second to disorient them for a few seconds if need be. Also tranquillizer guns.'

'Guns?' Hatty asked.

'Look, I said we're not going to ask you to kill anyone,' Jim said. 'You're children. You're excellent spies, but you're not killers. I don't want you out there doing that. So you knock them out. That's it.'

'And what do we have to do?'

'Surround them wherever they stop tonight. Make sure they're all there. Knock them out with the tranquillizer guns, then alert the Polish authorities to what's been going on, without implicating yourselves or the UK. Look, you've used high explosives in training. Done this kind of recce. It's not so different from your training, except that, rather than killing them, you'll just be knocking them out for a few hours.'

The children continued to stare at Jim.

Jim stared back. 'Nobody else can do this but you,' he said. 'You can see that, can't you?'

'Yes,' said Kester. He knew that this mission would push the Squad's skills and bravery to the limit, but it had to be done. It was up to them to save the England team.

'But before all that,' Lily said, 'there's the small matter of playing football against the best youth team in the world.'

ENGLAND V. SPAIN

At the end of the Spain match – and after shaking hands with the Spanish players – the whole England youth team collapsed on to the ground. The game had been impossibly hard. So hard they had not noticed the stadium with its towering stands and row on row of glass-fronted executive boxes, only the rectangle of grass they'd been playing
on.

From the first minute the Spanish team had passed the ball around so fast it was dizzying and the children had felt like they were playing Barcelona on a PlayStation World Class setting. The England defenders hadn't had a second to think. They'd needed to watch every player and every ball for forty-five minutes. Then for another forty-five.

They had run and blocked and run and tackled and run and fouled and run and hoofed. In goal Adnan had been immense. He'd stopped shot after shot, having gained confidence from the first game.

It was strange. Something had changed. And whatever that something was it meant that now they were a pretty good team, all eleven of them.

There had been only one goal between kick-off and the final whistle. It had come from a mistake by Adnan. He'd bowled the ball out to Kester on the right, but a Spanish attacker had read the move and intercepted. Suddenly it had been one Spanish striker against Adnan in his goal.

Adnan had decided he had to try to take control of the situation, rather than be passive. Or at least pretend to. But what should he do? How many goalkeepers had survived a one-on-one with a Spanish striker by using ordinary goalkeeping techniques?

Not many.

So Adnan had run out of the goal at the Spanish player, which was not what the striker had been expecting. And Adnan had seen it in the striker's eyes. A question mark.

Doubt!

Adnan had got into the Spanish striker's head. He'd seized the moment and lunged at him; the boy had panicked, scuffing the ball past Adnan. Adnan had looked back to see the ball trickling towards the net, so he'd leaped at it and tucked it into his chest, just as the entire Spanish team had come thundering down to knock in the loose ball, closely followed by the entire England team. Everyone except Rio, who was standing on the halfway line.

Adnan had spotted him and – without hesitating – hurled the ball half the length of the pitch to him. Rio had chested it down, turned, taken five or six paces with the ball at his feet, had seen the Spanish keeper coming off his line and hit it skywards.

The ball had sailed over the keeper, a white dot against the blue, then powered down and into the net.

Goal. An amazing goal.

England 1 Spain 0.

And that was how the game had finished.

In the heap of collapsed post-match English bodies, one figure moved. It was the team captain, Rio, making his way over to Adnan. He put his arm out to the keeper, hauled him off the ground and shook his hand.

Adnan couldn't believe what was happening: Rio was as excited as a child at Christmas.

'You were awesome today,' Rio said. Then he turned to the rest of the team. 'You all were. I can't believe what we've just done. We've beaten the best team in the world. And that means . . . that means . . . I can't believe it.' He was jumping around like an excited puppy now. 'We're in the final. We're going to meet Rooney and Theo and Joe Hart and Rio . . . Rio Ferdinand!'

'Who have we got next, Rio?' Kester asked, trying to calm him down.

'Russia.'

'Russia?' Hatty, Kester and Adnan said the word together.

'Yeah,' Rio replied, looking puzzled. 'What's wrong with them? They'll be a lot easier than Spain.'

'Oh, nothing,' Lily said, smiling.

IN THE CHURCH

After a good training session and lunch the next day, the players gathered in the entertainment room, everyone sitting in groups, talking and resting, except Georgia who was on her own, texting.

Lily was feeling tense. Really tense. She didn't like just sitting around at the best of times. All she could think about was that tonight the Squad had their most serious and dangerous mission ever, where they might actually have to attack people, something they'd never been asked to do before.

There was too much adrenalin going round her system: she had to do something.

'What shall we do?' she muttered, not sure if it was to the others or just to herself. No one answered.

'Where's Jim?' Kester asked after another minute.

'He's gone out somewhere,' Lily replied, shrugging.

For Lily, the room was creaking with boredom now. She watched Kester staring at the ceiling, then back at her. Lily could feel so much tension rising in her, she felt sick. She decided she would go for a run to burn it off. That was the answer. She stood up, ready to tell everyone her plan.

Then Kester made a suggestion. 'Let's go into the city centre.'

'Yeah,' Lesh said quickly.

'Great,' Lily agreed, having abandoned her idea for a run.

'Can I come?' Johnny asked.

One hour later, a tram deposited Lily, Lesh, Kester and Johnny in the centre of Krakow, one of Europe's most beautiful cities. Adnan and Hatty had stayed at the hotel, Hatty having pointed out that it was a good idea if the Squad didn't always hang around as a group.

Krakow was all arches and towers and narrow back streets, buildings made of painted wood. The kind of place parents get really excited about. There were weird sculptures scattered around the city, including one of a massive hollow head on its side next to a row of cafes in the main square.

In the far corner of the square was a cathedral, two towers against the bright blue sky. As bells sounded in the tower, Lily gazed up at it, smiling. She liked their sound as they pealed round the square.

That was when she saw the flash. A glimpse of orange in a tiny window at the top of the tower. It was the kind of thing they'd been trained to spot: if you are out in the wild and you see a flash from a hillside, it could be the telescopic sights of a high-velocity rifle targeting you, or someone in trouble using a mirror to get your attention.

Lily stared up at the tower, adjusting her eyes to the brightness of the sky. As she looked, she heard the noise of a trumpet sounding and she smiled. That was what the flash was. The brassy orange colour was the end of the trumpet.

'What's with the trumpet?' she asked Lesh, thinking he'd know because he was from Poland. But it was Johnny who answered.

'It's a tradition,' he said quickly, holding up a book. 'I read about it in this guide to Krakow. There was an attack on Krakow in the old days and a trumpeter was sounding the warning from the tower of the Mariacki Church, but he was shot dead by an enemy arrow. Since then, they've sounded a trumpet from that tower every fifteen minutes, day and night, to mark his death.'

'Wow,' Lily said. 'That's amazing.'

Johnny smiled.

They walked around the city, stopping for some food, looking in shops. Every lamp post seemed to have a Euro 2012 banner on it and every shop window had some sort of display related to football, even chemists and cafes.

Lily noticed that every fifteen minutes the trumpet sounded, just like Johnny had said it would. But she'd had enough of shops and walking. She'd thought of something she wanted to do: light a candle for Rob.

'Can we go to the cathedral?' she asked.

'Do we have to?' said Lesh. 'No offence, but stuff like that's boring.'

Kester was looking the other way, clearly not wanting to go with Lily.

'I'll come,' Johnny said.

'Thanks, Johnny,' Lily smiled.

So Lily and Johnny walked over to the cathedral. It was made of red and white bricks and had two towers, one taller than the other, with a huge entrance door between them.

'I love the trumpeter,' Lily said.

'Me too,' Johnny agreed.

They walked in through the cathedral door, their eyes adjusting to the dark and ill-lit interior after the bright sunshine outside. They saw painted pillars, gold chandeliers hanging down from chains and white marble statues.

Johnny had stopped chatting. He was staring at the ceiling, a bright blue with gold stars reflecting the light of a thousand candles.

They walked over to a bank of candles, some lit and shining. Lily slipped a coin into the box, took a candle out of a tray and lit it. Then she closed her eyes and thought for a few seconds about Rob. As she did all this, Johnny said nothing. He just smiled at her.

'Are you looking forward to the final?' Lily asked him in a whisper.

Johnny nodded vigorously and whispered back: 'I am. I'd love to win it. I've never won in a final before . . .'

Lily looked around the cathedral as Johnny spoke. She always did this in unfamiliar places, so she knew the inside of a building in case something dangerous suddenly happened. It was a habit she had got into. She saw that there was another entrance to the cathedral, one for people who wanted to pray as well as the one for tourists. Near that, a door led to a stone staircase. She wondered if that was the one that led up the taller tower, where the trumpeter might go.

'Never won a final?' Lily asked, her thoughts back on Johnny.

'No. I mean, I've played for big sides. I was at Liverpool for a bit. But not . . .'

Lily knew that Johnny was still talking, but all her attention was now on a man at the front of the pews. One of the things the Squad had been trained to do was identify a person from their body shape and the way they carried themselves without seeing their face, even if they were in disguise.

'. . . think we make a really good team . . .'

Lily tried to take in what Johnny was saying while looking at the man.

'. . . with your defending . . .'

It was Jim. She knew it. And he was praying.

Johnny smiled. 'Who have you played for?'

'I was with the Lincoln Imps girls' team,' Lily replied, using the backstory she'd been given by Julia.

Lily wanted to get closer to Jim to double-check that it was him. 'I need to pray,' she said to Johnny quickly.

'Oh . . . OK,' Johnny said. 'Feel free. I'll just hang around here.'

Lily put her hand on Johnny's arm and smiled. 'Thank you.'

Then she approached the man and saw that it was Jim, alone in a pew, his hands together, praying. And it made her think. Was Jim religious? Had he ever mentioned churches or anything like that?

No. Only that time he'd said he wasn't particularly religious. But what did that mean? Here she was, after all, liking being in a church and she wouldn't describe herself as religious. Maybe he was praying for the Squad: in a few hours they'd be on their most dangerous mission yet.

ASSAULT

None of the children spoke as they waited for Jim's briefing. They just stood with their backs against the helicopter, staring at their kitbags.

They were not quiet because of nerves: they were quiet because this was their toughest mission ever – the first in which they would be required to attack an enemy – and they wanted to be completely focused.

Minutes before, Jim had spelled out again what they were required to do, spreading a map out on the fuselage of the helicopter. They had gone through everything in painstaking detail.

'You'll be dropped at the side of a lake about a hundred kilometres away. The journey will take little more than twenty minutes. By the lake you'll find a small Zodiac inflatable boat. You need to use it to reach this island here, three kilometres east of the landing area. The motor on the boat is fully submerged and very quiet. From the island, I want you to snorkel one and half kilometres to this point here on the beach. Your targets – Svid and the two others – are in the woods fifty to sixty metres back. I want you to get within twenty metres of them, then using night vision, your grenades and tranquillizer guns, I want you to attack. They arrived there at 20:30 hours and have not moved since 22:40. It's 23:50 hours now. You will make contact at 01:40. Any questions?'

'You've already briefed us about how to attack the camp,' Kester replied. 'We've got the satellite and drone data coming in live, so we can see any changes once we're about to go in. I think we're OK. Team?'

Kester faced the other four, who all replied with sharp nods.

'Because this is so dangerous,' Jim said, 'I'll be in radio contact at all times via the satellite phone. I'm going back to the city now to oversee the England team's appearance in Krakow tomorrow, to meet and greet the local people. You know: PR shots, that sort of thing.'

Then the helicopter's blades began to turn and Jim looked ready to leave.

'Good luck,' he said. 'I know you can do this. You're a fantastic team. Just use what you've learned.'

He shook each of them by the hand. And then he was gone.

The helicopter moved swiftly through the night. Lily looked down and saw a hundred million trees beneath her in the dark. It was black down there. Blacker than normal. And in her mind, turning and turning, there was an unease, something about this mission that didn't feel right.

But it was too late to discuss that now. The helicopter had stopped moving forward at speed and was dropping slowly towards a river to a height of twenty metres, where the Squad quickly grabbed their kit and descended on wires to the ground.

Now they had to get through two kilometres of dense woodland. Lesh navigated, using his GPS equipment. They had luminous strips on the backs of their baseball caps. In addition, Lily and Adnan set down a series of small illuminated sticks on their chosen path. They would be able to use these to help them find their way back to the helicopter, after the mission.

'It's a bit like Hansel and Gretel this,' Adnan whispered to Lily. 'I wonder what the witch is like.'

Lily shoved Adnan and smiled. She decided she liked having him around.

Eventually, after struggling through the woods, they saw a light, the stars shining off the surface of a very black lake.

Kester and Lesh located the boat and snorkelling gear quickly and prepared the boat for their short journey to the island.

'This is a beauty,' Lesh said. 'We trained in one last week, remember? Look, the engine is submerged, so the sound waves it gives off go through the water and don't skim across the lake, giving us away. It's –'

'Can you operate it, Lesh?' Hatty cut in impatiently.

'Of course . . .'

'Then just get it in the water!'

Lesh didn't respond to Hatty. She was tetchy, which meant she was nervous and he knew it was best to leave her alone.

Minutes later, the Squad were on a river, allowing its currents to pull their boat towards the lake. On the far side of the lake from the river mouth, less than five kilometres away now, was the target: the camp and the three men the Squad had been tracking all week. But they couldn't see it. It was as dark as it could be, clouds covering the moon and stars.

Once they had drifted into the lake, Lesh started up the engine. They could hardly hear it even though they were sitting right next to it.

Only Lesh could see where they were going, but his night-vision goggles barely showed the lake, island and the distant beach, there was so little light. For the others the sky above them was as impenetrably black as the water beneath them.

The journey was quick and carried out in absolute silence.

When they arrived at the island, Lesh tapped Kester on the shoulder. Kester immediately started to hand out the snorkels and masks without speaking.

Words would carry across the water and, above the sound of the ripples and waves of the lake, might alert the men to their presence.

The four other members of the Squad took their snorkelling gear as Lesh secured the boat on the far side of the island to the beach and quickly set up his SpyPad to control the drone. He did it in seconds, moving the drone out of the circle it was making over the woods to focus its cameras down on the target. It was an easy task, just like doing it on a video simulator. But, because it was real, Lesh felt amazing. One of his dreams was coming true: he was operating a drone, using a body-heat scanner to see where the men were and what they were doing.

The Squad watched him as he did this, waiting for his verdict.

'Strange,' Lesh whispered.

'What is it?'

'There's nothing registering on the body-heat sensor.'

'Use the night vision,' Hatty murmured.

Lesh changed the application on his SpyPad and set up the drone's night vision. He shook his head.

'Nothing,' he whispered. 'It's like it's empty. No fires. No bodies. They've gone.'

Lesh looked at Kester's camouflaged face.

'They can't have gone,' Kester whispered.

'Or they want us to think they've gone,' Lesh went on.

'They were here an hour ago. Half an hour ago. We saw them from the drone before we left Jim.'

Kester shook his head. 'We need to find out for sure. We'll all swim over there. Me, Adnan and Hatty will advance slowly on foot. Lily and Lesh can wait on the shoreline. We have to sort this. Now.'

Kester looked at Hatty. She nodded quickly: she would do exactly what her leader had told her to do.

So the five children fitted their snorkels and dipped into the lake, slowly and carefully, without making a single splashing noise, letting the cold black water envelop them. Lesh tried not to think of what could be under the water because he knew that was all in his mind and that the real danger lay a kilometre and a half away, on the shore.

Then they swam, five abreast, just under the surface, their muscles warming as they began to move more easily. They had no idea what they would face when they arrived at the beach.

INTO THE DARK

The Squad emerged from the water less than a hundred metres from the target, acutely aware that it could be some kind of trap. An ambush. But there was no sign of human life for kilometres either by the naked eye or using satellites and drones.

At first, they crawled from the water, keeping low. When they reached the cover of a large outcrop of rocks, they stopped to consult Lesh's SpyPad and remove their snorkelling gear. Still nothing: no sign of man. Nor beast.

Adnan knew someone had to move forward and put themselves at risk to clear the way for the others. He tapped Kester on the shoulder and gestured that he would go up the beach, on point, meaning he would lead the assault. Kester nodded his agreement.

'Lesh will keep check on the SpyPad,' Kester whispered.

Kester indicated that Hatty should slot in right behind him, armed with the tranquillizer gun.

This was the plan for Kester, Hatty and Adnan.

Lesh and Lily would monitor events on the SpyPad from the beach. They would maintain radio silence throughout, unless there was an emergency.

Soon the three disappeared into the eerie blackness of the woods, meaning all Lily and Lesh could see of them were three red dots on a screen, images coming back from the drone circling above them.

Lesh was sure that they were alone and this was just an easy reconnaissance mission. If the men from the quarry were still there, they would have showed up on the screen. But still the tension was unbearable. He felt his mouth go dry and he wished he could take a sip of water, but he knew he had to focus. Neither he nor Lily spoke as they watched the three red blobs circle the target area, wait five minutes, then edge towards it.

'What if the men are hiding there?' Lily asked Lesh.

'They can't be. They'd show up. They'd need to be buried at least a metre underground for the drone to miss the heat of their bodies.'

Lily nodded. She felt a little better. Maybe this mission was going to be OK after all. She watched the red dots advance closer to the target area, but, however much she tried to tell to herself that it was safe, she still felt a deep and insistent fear.

The woods around them were motionless, the birds silent. There were no more shufflings and snufflings in among the branches and on the ground.

'What's that?' Lesh's voice was too loud. He dropped the SpyPad on the floor in shock.

'What?' Lily said, staring at him.

'I saw something,' Lesh said, picking up the SpyPad. 'Look!'

On the monitor, two additional red blobs were moving slowly towards the three blobs that Lesh and Lily knew were their friends.

Lesh handed Lily the SpyPad and swiftly spoke into his watch. 'Incoming bodies. Two. To your east.'

'Copy.' Kester's voice sounded shrill.

Then Lily and Lesh watched in horror as their three friends began to move at speed away from the threat, back to the water.

'They must have been hiding,' Lily said. 'Waiting. It's a trap.'

Lesh and Lily carried on watching. The two red blobs had speeded up too and were getting closer, moving incredibly fast through the trees. Impossibly fast.

'They're closing in,' Lily said, panicking, as she grabbed Kester's bag, pulling out one of the two stun grenades he'd left with them. 'How can they move so fast?'

Lily was not really aware of what she was doing. Instinct told her to run up the shore towards the danger and not away from it.

She advanced until she saw Hatty, Kester and Adnan coming towards her. Then, the second they passed her, their shoulders brushing, Lily hurled the grenade, expecting to be hit by a bullet at any moment.

Only Lily saw what was happening, while the others ran for cover and Lesh observed it all on his screen.

For a second the grenade caused vivid flashes which illuminated the woods and the two figures chasing her friends.

They were not men. They were wolves. And as soon as the grenade went off, they turned and ran back into the woods.

For the first minute after the wolves had run away, the children were utterly speechless. They eyed each other silently.

Hatty shook her head, then put her hand on Lily's knee and smiled. Lily smiled back.

'Was that . . . ?' Hatty asked.

Lily nodded, then changed the subject quickly. 'What did you see in the woods?'

'There's barely anything there,' Kester gasped, getting his breath back. 'We searched it with a torch. You wouldn't know anyone had been there if it wasn't for some patches of flattened grass and some snapped branches. And . . .'

'And the container?' Lily asked.

'That was there,' Kester replied.

'And?'

'And it was empty,' Kester confessed. 'No rocket launcher.'

There was a wind now, coming gently from the east. The trees had started to rustle, as though a storm was coming.

'So where have they gone? Where have they taken the rocket launcher?' Lily asked. 'Why have they just disappeared off the radar?'

'We can't answer that,' Hatty said.

'Wait!' Adnan spluttered. 'Do you remember Jim said he had to sort the security for England's walkabout in the main square tomorrow?'

Kester nodded.

'That's what they're hitting,' Adnan said urgently. 'They're not attacking the England training base or their hotel in two days. They've gone now because they're hitting the walkabout in a few hours.'

'We don't know that,' said Kester.

'Well, call Jim on the satellite phone,' Hatty insisted. 'Now!'

Kester looked at Lesh, then nodded. Lesh started to fumble in his waterproof kitbag to find their satellite phone. He dialled and gave it to Kester.

Kester put it to his ear and his face paled. 'There's a monotone.'

'Is it out of range?' Lesh asked, taking the phone off Kester.

'What?' Hatty asked impatiently.

'No, that's not it,' Lesh said. 'He's turned it off.'

'But he never does that,' Lily said. 'He said he'd be there for us. He said if he did that then . . .'

'Then something's seriously wrong,' Hatty added. 'Maybe they've got Jim. We don't know anything.'

'Try Julia,' Kester ordered. 'If we can't talk to Jim, then we have to try Julia.'

They all watched Lesh's face as he dialled Julia's number. And they all saw his face look even graver after a few seconds.

'It's dead too, isn't it?' Hatty said.

'Same tone,' said Lesh. 'We're on our own.'

Kester started moving towards the water. 'Come on!' he shouted. 'We have to get back across the water and into the helicopter.'

'What?' Adnan said.

'We've got three hours to get out of these woods, into Krakow and to the main square. If Jim's not there for whatever reason, then we're the only ones who can stop the attack.'

LEAVING IT LATE

Once they were across the lake and out of the water, the Squad ran as hard as they could through the woods. No more creeping around: they had to get back to the helicopter pick-up point fast. The men they'd been tracking were long gone. Gone to Krakow to kill the England football team. Perhaps.

None of them spoke as they ran, tree branches whipping across their faces, their feet sinking into deep mud holes. They fell over stones, cut their hands, twisted their ankles, but they ran on. They had no choice.

The return was made easier by the illuminated sticks they'd left on the track. They collected them all as they ran. This time, Lily noticed, Adnan did not make a Hansel and Gretel joke.

As they approached the helicopter landing area, coming up through the trees, Kester spoke into his mic.

'Two minutes off,' he said, hoping he'd hear the

helicopter pilot reply. If he was out of contact, they'd really be in trouble.

'Roger,' a voice crackled on his radio. And immediately Kester heard the *thump-thump-thump* of the blades and saw the trees beginning to be tossed about.

By the time the five of them were underneath the chopper, the blades were a blur in the night and the forest was thrashing about like a cyclone had just hit.

They went up one by one, swinging through the forest like they were in some spectacular amusement park.

On board, Kester was starting to feel panicky and he knew that was the worst thing to be as leader. He turned to look at the pilot, hoping he would have some information.

The pilot looked back. 'I've lost contact with Jim Sells, Kester. But only after he asked me to return to Krakow. But your commander in the UK, Julia, overruled him when I queried it with her. What are your orders?'

Kester's heart sank. 'I can't get him either,' he said. Then his mind started working overtime.

'Julia overruled him?'

'Yes. I radiocd her for a confirmation and then, when she told me to stay with you, Jim went quiet. I've not heard a thing since.'

Kester shook his head. *What's that all about?*

'So?' the pilot said. His hand was on the controls, holding the helicopter in position.

So what? Kester said to himself. *So what do we do now? The men have vanished. Jim is out of contact.* What was he supposed to say to the pilot? Shouldn't he be the one offering solutions?

And then his mind cleared and he understood: the pilot was waiting for orders. But not from Jim. From him. He was in charge now and he had to lead, to make the decisions.

Kester swallowed. 'We need to get into Krakow. The centre. Without being seen.'

The pilot smiled.

'Can you do that?' Kester urged.

'I can,' the pilot replied. 'But hold on tight.'

None of them looked at the view this time. As they changed into fresh clothes and wiped the muddy water and cam cream off, the black mountains stood high and still, the rivers ran through the night and a million creatures ate and slept and moved from one place to another.

But the Squad were too busy to look. They lay on the floor of the chopper, looking at a map of Krakow. Planning.

'When we get to the city centre, we have to split up,' Kester said, taking control. 'We have to assume that the terrorists will be coming into the city one way or another. We have to anticipate where and be there to stop them.'

'OK,' said Hatty.

'When the England team enter the main square, there will be thousands of people there. Most of them just want to get a look at Wayne Rooney and Theo Walcott. The only chance we have of stopping an attack on them is by spotting the man who surprised us.'

'Lesh, show us the picture I took,' Lily suggested.

Lesh displayed the photo of the man. Svidrigaylov.

'It's been enhanced,' he said. 'So it's clearer. And this is a photo of him from a couple of years ago. But, as you can see, he has different facial hair now. So try to remember both images.'

The others nodded. They had committed his face to memory. Now all they had to do was find him.

'But can I just ask?' Hatty said. 'Why don't we simply call the police or the army? Or the England team? Warn them?'

There was a moment's silence. It was a blindingly obvious question.

Adnan supplied the answer that everyone understood quite well. 'Because if we tell anyone, then the authorities in Poland – and probably Russia – will know exactly what's going on and who we are and it will blow this and every future mission.'

'And because Jim has said we're not to,' Lily added.

'And that's it too,' Kester said. We don't know

where Jim is. He could be back at the hotel waiting for us. He could have been taken. I have serious doubts. We just don't know.'

'Julia then?'

'I've tried a couple of times since we were on the beach,' Lesh said. 'The line's dead.'

'So we have to go it alone,' Hatty said.

'That's right,' Kester agreed, knowing it was a gamble. Any choice they made now was a gamble. This was never meant to be easy.

As the helicopter approached Krakow, the pilot moved in low over the Wisła River. The base of the helicopter was almost touching the surface, and water was being thrown up on to the windows as if they were travelling in a speedboat. It wasn't light yet, so they skimmed into the city unseen.

The Squad sat in darkness and absolute silence, readying themselves for the search of Krakow. None of them was nervous. Even though they were about to go into an unknown situation that they didn't have orders for, they were all grinning. This helicopter ride and the prospect of doing what they were about to do was suddenly too exciting.

Lesh pointed ahead. 'There,' he said, 'that place called Wawel Hill.'

They all looked. Ahead of them, looming over the river, was a fortified hill, topped by a cathedral and other buildings, one of Krakow's most famous land-marks. Lights flashed by from occasional cars beside the river.

'You need to decide how you want to land,' the pilot said, leaning back to address the children.

'What are the options?' Kester asked.

'Three options. One, land by the river. It's the safest, but you're most likely to be seen by someone who may report us to the authorities.

'Two, I hover over the fortress and you go down on your wires. That's effective and not really danger-ous, but leaves us in the air a long time, so again we may be spotted.'

'And three?' Kester asked.

'Three. This helicopter is the most spectacular thing in the air. It can get in and out of small spaces, landing and leaving again within seconds, so fast that people won't believe it was a helicopter. There's a huge lawn up there at the centre of Wawel Hill. It's perfect, surrounded by walls. I can get the chopper in unseen. The security guards will be asleep or in their rooms, so will probably miss us. It's dangerous in that there's a one per cent chance we might crash.'

'One per cent is nothing,' Hatty said to Kester.

'I agree. Let's take option three,' said Kester. 'We're going to have to take risks and if we can get in there without being spotted, all the better.'

Before Kester had finished speaking the helicopter rose in a steep curve, as if it was climbing the walls of the fort. They were all thrown back into their seats, like when a plane takes off, but with much more power. Then the helicopter seemed to stop in mid-air, leaving them feeling they were suspended there, before it dropped on to the lawn with barely a bump.

It was such a quick ending to the flight that the children just sat there, dumbfounded and disbelieving.

'Is that it? Have we landed?'

'Go now!' the pilot shouted.

Kester ushered the four other Squad members out of the chopper and on to the lawn where they sprinted for cover. As they did so, the helicopter rose then dropped over the wall and back down towards the river.

Kester crouched with the others at the side of a building. They were breathless and used the time to get air into their lungs and oxygen into their blood in case they had to run again.

After a few seconds, they saw two men coming quickly from a doorway. Security guards, as the pilot had said. The guards looked around, confused. They'd obviously heard something, but by the time they'd come outside, the helicopter was gone and the children were hidden.

Kester couldn't believe what the helicopter had just done. It was almost a miracle. But now the Squad needed a real miracle.

They were back in Krakow with a couple of hours to stop a group of three terrorists from attacking the England football team. And they still had no idea where their commander was and what he was doing.

THE SACRIFICE

Kester decided to send each of the Squad members to one of Krakow's important transport hubs. It was six in the morning and they had three hours before the England team rolled into town at 9 a.m. Only at 8.30 a.m. would they gather in the main square, which was called Rynek Główny. This was the usual procedure: try to spot possible threats where they could arrive and, if you miss them, converge on the site of the possible attack.

Lesh had continued to try to contact Jim by satellite, mobile phone and radio. But there was still no reply. Kester decided that they were on their own with no time to worry about where their commander was. They had a job to do. If he turned up, then great. If not, so be it. They could worry about what had happened to him later.

They studied the map together to discuss the places they should monitor, sitting by the river at the foot of the walls of the fortress. They looked at places where people would come into the city this morning. Shop workers. Students. Football fans. Council employees. Tourists. And – maybe – terrorists.

They chose carefully.

One, the central train station. Kester remembered footage from terror attacks in the UK. They were always the same: film images of men arriving at stations with rucksacks, ready to create havoc. He'd deploy Lily there.

Two, a huge bridge – Powstańców Śląskich – over the river that brought traffic in from south-east Poland. Kester chose to send Lesh there. He knew vehicles. He'd be able to spot anything unusual.

Three, John Paul II International Airport, where they'd arrived. It was unlikely the men would come in by air, but Kester could not rule it out. That was a job for Adnan.

Four, the Wisła River. It was the last way in. By boat. Hatty's post.

'What about you?' Hatty asked. 'Where are you going?'

Kester paused for a second, then changed his mind. 'New plan,' he said. 'Lily, you do the other station, the Zabłocie Station. They might come in there and walk into the city. Trains from the east arrive there first. I'll cover the Central Station.'

Lily nodded.

'I want radio contact every ten minutes from each of you,' Kester finished. 'If any of you see something, I'll decide who to deploy where. I'll keep trying to contact Jim. We'll leave our posts and gather round the back of the Mariacki Church at eight thirty. OK?'

Between them, the Squad saw over thirty thousand faces coming into Krakow city centre that morning.

They watched for unusual behaviour, people carrying objects that were out of the ordinary. Rucksacks. People not walking and talking like others. This was something they had been trained for. Once you'd done it a few times, you got an eye for it.

But today they saw nothing except hundreds of men, women and children getting off trains and buses and out of cars, standing under the huge banners promoting Euro 2012 and its sponsors.

Between 07:30 and 08:15 Kester radioed them all. They had seen nothing and no one. 'Come back to the Mariacki Church,' he said. 'Abort stage one. We have to pursue stage two.'

Stage two was to search the city centre before the England team arrived. If Svid and his friends were in Krakow now, they would be in the centre, ready to do what they were planning.

The centre of Krakow had changed radically in the couple of hours the Squad had been at their posts.

Now there were thousands of people standing behind crowd-control barriers, including hundreds of schoolchildren and dozens of police officers. *It looks so unreal that it seems like a film set,* Lily thought. *For a disaster movie.*

'What now?' Hatty asked, once they were all together.

Kester felt a stab of panic in his heart. He was supposed to be leading this operation and so far they'd come up with nothing. He felt like he was failing, that the England team were about to be attacked and he had done nothing to stop it. He heard the trumpeter playing in the cathedral tower.

Maybe, he thought, *Hatty was the right choice for leader. Maybe she would have delivered results.* But he had to stop thinking like that. He had a job to do.

To stop the attack.

This wasn't about him being leader: it was about the footballers and their families and the hundreds of schoolchildren standing in the square. And anyway, most spies and agents spent days, weeks, months watching for people, preventing attacks. How was he supposed to nail it in a morning?

Kester saw the other four looking at him. Waiting. The noise of the crowd was growing, adding to the Squad's tension.

'We have to decide something,' he said.

'Decide what?' asked Hatty.

'If we want to jeopardize the Squad,' Kester explained. 'Because if we alert the authorities now, our cover is blown for future missions. It's a lot to risk.'

'The alternative risk is to the whole England team,' Lily countered.

'Exactly,' Kester said. 'We've agreed not to go to the authorities, but maybe we need to change that plan now. And we have to decide without Jim.'

'Still nothing?' Lesh asked.

'It's like he's vanished off the face of the earth,' said Kester.

'I think the England team have to take priority,' Adnan broke in.

'Me too,' Lily agreed.

'I'm not so sure,' Hatty argued. 'Then the Polish authorities will know about us. Maybe the Russians. We'll never work again. We'll be known by security services around the world, just like all the adults were. Everything special that we can do to protect the UK will be blown. That'll be it.'

Then Lesh knelt forward. 'We have to do it, Hatty. Why did we all agree to do this sort of thing anyway? Why are we in the Squad?'

Hatty didn't answer, so Lesh carried on. 'Why do we put our lives at risk to stop terrorists? Why do we work for the government? Why don't we go to school and live in a children's home and just read spy books like Johnny, instead of being spies?'

'Because of that morning,' Hatty said in a low voice.

'Exactly,' said Lesh. 'We do what we do because one day, two years ago, our parents were shot dead in front of our eyes. It was horrendous and impossible to live with. And because we had no one else, we came together and we decided to do everything we could to make sure no other children lose their parents like we did, because of so-called terrorists. That's what we do. And we'd do it whether we were working for the government or not. Wouldn't we?'

Hatty sighed and closed her eyes.

'And how many of the England players are dads?' Lesh went on.

'Nine of them. Fifteen kids in all.' Now her eyes were open. 'OK,' she said, her voice wobbling. 'We go to the police. Now. We should have done it hours ago.'

'But are they going to take us seriously?' Adnan asked. 'A bunch of kids saying, "Stop everything. Someone is going to murder the England football team."'

Kester smiled and made a quick decision. 'Well, if anyone can do it, Hatty can. She'll be the most convincing.'

'I need Lesh too,' Hatty said.

'Of course,' Kester agreed, knowing she was right.

Kester, Adnan and Lily watched Hatty and Lesh from a hundred metres away.

They saw them approach a pair of policewomen, who were standing next to a man wearing a military uniform and carrying a machine gun. They could only just see them through crowds of football fans and other people who were walking in the square. At first, Hatty was talking calmly. Then, after some head-shaking from the policewomen, she became more animated, waving her arms about. That was when the man with the machine gun turned and said something to Lesh.

Kester looked at Lily to see if she'd been able to lip-read, but Lily shook her head.

Another crowd of people walked between the boys and girls. When they'd passed, Kester saw Hatty coming towards him, but she didn't have the look of disappointment on her face that he expected: she looked shocked; there was no sign of Lesh and now Hatty was running, like someone was coming after her.

What was this?

And where was Lesh?

Kester started to panic. Maybe the police weren't police at all. Maybe they were security forces. Maybe everything was about to go even more badly wrong.

Then, while still running, her eyes on Kester, he saw Hatty speak into her mic. But he could hear nothing.

'Lily, can you hear her?'

'No,' Lily said. 'Our comms are down. I can't believe it.'

But there was no more time to worry about mics and comms. Hatty was right there in front of them.

'The police think we're just stupid kids,' she said. 'It's a no go . . . but forget that . . . Lesh spotted Svid . . . he was with the two other men, all wearing England tops . . . but not proper ones . . . rubbish replica ones that no real England fan would be seen dead in. He's gone after Svid. In there.' Hatty rolled her eyes towards the church. 'The other two went that way . . . and Svid . . . Svid's carrying a long tube in a bag.'

Kester's mind moved into a high gear. The rocket launcher.

'Lily,' he said. 'Go after Lesh. He's seen Svid go into the cathedral. The rest of us will see if we can stop the other two.'

A second later, they were gone: five children chasing down three terrorists, hoping they could avert a disaster that no one else knew was about to unfold.

THE FALL

When Lily reached the cathedral, she spotted Lesh straight away.

There were two doors to enter the cathedral. One was marked 'For Prayer Only' and one further down the side was for tourists, the one that she'd gone through with Johnny the day before.

Lily had no idea which to use, but her instinct told her to go into the one that was not for tourists this time. She always trusted her gut reactions, so she slowed down and entered as if she was going in to pray. Lesh followed her.

Inside it was dark, in contrast to the bright sunshine outside. As her eyes became accustomed to the light, Lily saw two rows of people sitting on pews. More people standing. All facing a man dressed in religious robes, carrying out a service. Lily knew she had to blend in, to pretend she was there to pray, so she walked slowly, head down, making her way to the back row of pews, with Lesh right behind her.

Although she was looking down, she was still able to scan the church.

There was no sign of Svid. Nothing. Only the massive Jesus, arms outstretched as if he was trying to warn them.

As she looked around, Lily was thinking about Jim. How she'd seen him here praying, but that he'd said he wasn't religious and now he had disappeared. Her mind was coming to some sort of conclusion, a thought emerging. Then she heard the bells going off in the tower and caught Lesh's eye. She sighed and shook her head. 'We've lost him,' she whispered.

Lesh frowned. 'Now what?'

Lily scanned the inside of the cathedral again. She had to get her mind back on to Svid. 'You get to the other door. Wait there. Speak into your mic if you see him. I'll cover this end. OK?'

Lesh nodded and walked away.

As she watched him, Lily's heart stopped, her eyes on the door that went up to the tower. The trumpeter's tower.

And she knew where Svid was.

She'd not heard the trumpet after the cathedral bells.

And, as the thought came to her, she heard something else. Applause. Applause coming from outside. It was the England team. They were entering the square.

164

Suddenly Lily understood everything. Svid was in the tower. He'd disabled the trumpeter somehow. He had a rocket launcher. And the England coach was coming into his range.

'LESH!' she shouted across the cathedral. 'UP THE TOWER!'

The two women praying in front of Lily jumped visibly, then angry faces turned to her. And now the priest was moving towards her. Lily had broken church etiquette, but that didn't matter now. What mattered was getting up the tower.

Lily vaulted over the pews and hurdled a tomb. She was heading for the door she'd seen last time she came here. To the stairs. She could hear Lesh's boots pounding on the stone flags of the floor of the cathedral as he ran too. And shouting. Several voices shouting. Noises were coming from every angle, then echoing back from other angles again. But she shut it all out. The noise. The chaos. Even Lesh. Lily had one focus: get up the steps of the tower as swiftly as she could because she knew what was about to happen. The trumpeter had not blown, maybe for the first time in a century. It meant one thing: Svid was up there. And the only reason he was up there was to do something bad and he was going to do it now, just as the England team were arriving.

Lily kicked off her shoes, knowing she could run soundlessly in her socks, then took the steps three at a time. It was steep and it was hard, but all those years of fell-running with her dad were paying off now. She knew how to breathe, she knew how to move so that she had enough energy to be able to do something when she reached the top. For a second, she was distracted by the thought of her dad, the fell-runner, her missing hero. She hoped he'd be proud of her for this.

Soon the stone gave way to wooden steps. Lily ran through shadows and shafts of light, round and round the spiral staircase. She was so flooded with adrenalin that she could barely feel the effort of the climb. Lesh, she knew, would be a long way behind her.

Lily realized that she had reached the top of the tower when she saw the face staring straight back at her. It was on a wooden platform that marked the top of the tower. From the platform you could reach the four walls of the tower and the small windows that let light in from outside.

The face's two bulging eyes shocked her at first and she stepped back to defend herself. But it took less than a second for her brain to work it out. This was the trumpeter. Next to him, his trumpet. There was a pool of red-black liquid by his head. Blood.

He was dead.

Lily peered over the man's body and saw what she feared most. Svid was standing with his feet on the banisters above the platform, his body twisted at a strange angle, leaning over a huge drop down the inside of the tower, with a large tube projecting behind him.

Lily gasped inaudibly. There was no question what the tube was. It was the rocket launcher they'd known he would have and the man was aiming it out of the top window of the church — no doubt directly at the England team bus.

Lily could hear the noise of the crowd building. She knew the England team would be getting out of their coach to meet the locals.

No time to lose.

She crept towards Svid, about to try to pull him down. But then she thought again: what if he just kicked her away. She could hear Lesh a few flights below, running to help her. But he would not get there in time. She was the only one who could save the lives of the England players and those crowding around them. She tried to decide the best course of action. She had seconds. Less than seconds. He could pull the trigger and obliterate two dozen foot-ballers and lots of members of the public at any moment.

No time. No time. Decide.

Then her hand was grabbing for the trumpet, the glinting piece of brass on the floor. She put it to her lips and blew.

The noise it made was a shock even to Lily, bounc-ing around the small chamber of the bell tower.

Then Svid was dropping. It had worked. The noise

had shocked him so badly that he fell. At first, his fall felt slow, his hands grasping for something to hold on to, tipping, leaving the rocket launcher wedged in the window of the clock tower. Then his arms flailed out, making him look a bit like the huge Jesus down below in the cathedral, and his legs came up and he seemed to somersault, his head crunching against a huge chunk of stone. Then he was plummeting, fast and soundlessly down the inside of the tower, at least twenty metres to where the stone steps became wooden.

Lily gasped for a second time, terrified the falling man might hit her friend, and shouting, 'LESH . . . LOOK OUT!'

The noise of Svid hitting the ground below was not right.

Then another sound. Someone screaming.

'LESH?' she shouted.

There was no reply. She sprinted down the steps, frantic with worry about her friend. Thirty metres down she found Svid. He was lying with his arms and legs twisted underneath him, his head smashed open.

But she dismissed him from her thoughts. He was dead. And that was good. But it was Lesh she was worried about. Where was he? This was the place he should have been by her reckoning: right where the dead man was lying. And why was the wooden banister rail half torn off, if Svid was two metres away from it and hadn't actually fallen on it?

Lily knew the answer. It was obvious.

She stepped over the dead body to stare down to the bottom of the clock tower.

THE SCULPTURE

Kester, Adnan and Hatty ran across the square at the same time that Lily and Lesh entered the church. They had no idea where Svid's cronies were, so they needed to get to the other side fast.

But as the trio approached the far corner, Hatty, who was ahead, suddenly changed direction and ran to the side of a solitary tower that stood in one corner casting a great shadow across the square. The other two followed her unquestioningly, knowing she'd seen something.

'Is that them?' Kester asked, slightly breathless, pointing to two men wearing fake England tops in a cafe.

'It is,' Hatty confirmed.

'How are we going to get them?' Adnan asked. 'What can we do?'

'We need them in an enclosed space away from the public to use a grenade,' Kester said. 'A small room or an alleyway to use the tranquillizer gun.'

'That's impossible, so long as they're in the cafe,'

Hatty said. 'We have to wait for them to move on.'

'Let's at least get closer,' Adnan suggested. 'Take some photos of them.'

'Good idea,' said Kester.

'Look. See that sculpture thing there?' Adnan went on, pointing at a giant head sculpture on its side between the tower and the cafe. 'I saw it earlier. It's hollow and its eyes are facing the cafe. I'll go in it and take the photos from there.'

'OK,' Kester said, looking at the mic in his watch. 'We'll wait here and observe. Then we can always run back to help Lily if we're needed. I just wish I could get her on this thing. Can you, Hatty?'

'I'm getting nothing,' Hatty said. 'It's like our comms system is down. This is insane. I mean, we can't talk to Julia or Jim and now each other. Someone is doing this to us.'

'We just have to go on,' Kester said decisively.

'I agree,' said Adnan. 'I'll go and take some pictures of the men right now. Give me a grenade. Just in case.'

'In case of what?' Kester asked.

'In case I get lucky,' Adnan said.

Kester gave him a quizzical look, but still handed Adnan his rucksack, which contained the camera and the grenades. 'Take the whole bag,' he said.

Then the two of them watched as Adnan walked to the sculpture, keeping it between him and the two men, so they wouldn't see him approaching.

Once he was inside the sculpture, Adnan moved four or five metres to the far end and, on tiptoes, looked out of the higher eye. The gap was about the size of his head, perfect to put a camera through without being seen.

But not being seen wasn't part of Adnan's plan. He'd had an idea, something that might work, but that Kester would never agree to. Something that would involve the gas grenade.

Kester continued to watch the two men. They were smoking and drinking coffee under one of the cafe's sunshades that were fluttering in the light wind. He wondered if Adnan was getting good photographs. He hoped so: they could be invaluable when tracking the men down later.

Hatty was looking towards the church, checking to see any sign of what Lily and Lesh were up to. She hated this waiting around. Inaction was unbearable.

And then the men in the cafe stood suddenly and pointed at the sculpture that Adnan was hiding in. Before Kester could even tell Hatty, they were up out of their chairs, moving quickly towards Adnan. Kester expected to see Adnan come running out of the statue, but all he could see was the flashing of a camera. Adnan's camera. What was he doing? Was he mad? He was still taking photos as the men approached him.

'Hatty. Adnan needs us.'

But it was too late. As Kester and Hatty began to run towards their friend, they saw the two men were standing in the opening to the sculpture, that Adnan had moved right to the back and that now the men had gone in after him.

What was going on?

At the same time there were noises from the other side of the square. Applause. A crowd cheering.

'The England team must be coming in,' Kester said.

Then he heard Hatty scream and watched her running over towards Adnan and the men.

Wisps of gas were coming from the sculpture and people were backing away from it, some on their mobiles, others with scarves over their faces and mouths.

And Kester knew that both the terrorists and Adnan would now be out cold. Adnan had let off the gas grenade.

NEVER AGAIN

Lily sprinted down the next flight of steps, two images flashing through her mind.

The first was what she had just seen when she'd looked down: Lesh lying twenty metres below, unconscious on the stone slabs at the bottom of the church tower.

The second was Rob twisted in agony on the helicopter floor, just before he died. The hole in his leg. The blood. Knowing that he was going to die.

It could not be happening again. Lily wouldn't be able to bear it if Lesh was dead.

'Lesh! Lesh!' she shouted, finally reaching him, falling on her knees and grabbing his wrist.

But he did not reply. His face was pale and his lips had turned a strange colour, so Lily put her ear to his mouth to see if he was breathing.

He was not.

Lily opened his mouth to check for blockages. Nothing. Next she tipped his head back and breathed two long breaths into him. Basic life support came to her easily. Then she pumped thirty times on his chest, trying to start his heart again.

'It's OK, Lesh. It's going to be OK,' she sobbed.

As she worked, Lily felt a shadow fall over her. She looked up to see the priest who had been taking the church service. She breathed twice more into Lesh and saw the priest kneel beside her, put his hands together and murmur in a low voice.

After thirty more pumps to his chest, Lily moved in to see if Lesh was breathing, putting her ear next to his mouth and – after too long a gap – felt her ear tickled by his breath.

He was alive.

'Ambulance,' Lily said. 'He's breathing. But his pulse is weak.'

The man nodded, pulled an iPhone out of his cassock and immediately began dialling. No questions. He just did what she asked. Lily tried to smile at him to say thank you, but she knew her face was a twisted mass of tears and fears.

As the priest spoke to the ambulance service, Lily put Lesh into the recovery position, one leg straight, the other bent forward.

'The ambulance will be here in five minutes,' the priest said in Polish. 'Is there anything more I can do?'

'No. Thank you,' Lily said, comforted by the man's

kindness. And by the fact that, as well as being able to feel Lesh's pulse, she could also see his chest rising and falling.

But now that she had dealt with one problem, another surfaced. She could hear the crowds cheering the England first team outside again. How was the ambulance going to get through? Everyone would be making sure the famous footballers were comfortable and happy, not worrying about an emergency vehicle that they probably thought was there just in case a player needed it.

'Lesh?' she said. But there was no response. 'Lesh. I'm going outside to make sure the ambulance finds us. OK?'

Then she looked at the priest. 'Please. Hold his hand.'

The priest took Lesh's hand and Lily knew he was safe. So long as she could get this ambulance.

Outside the cathedral, in the bright piercing light, there was no sign of Kester, Adnan and Hatty. Only row after row of people and, next to a large luxury coach and behind some barriers, a group of men in blue suits. Lily recognized Theo Walcott, Joe Hart and Ashley Young right away. They looked strange in suits. She was so used to seeing them in their England or club strip.

Beyond them, Lily saw the ambulance pulling into the square. Its light was flashing blue and white, but its passage was blocked off by the crowd. How was she going to get the ambulance through? Then she noticed a large stone bollard and, without a thought, she leaped on to it.

Now she could see everything. The footballers. The crowd around them. The ambulance. She desperately wanted to call Kester, but their comms were still down. She needed another plan.

'Theo!' she shouted suddenly, targeting the nearest England player.

Theo Walcott didn't look round. A hundred people were shouting his name. Why would he look just at her? She had to get his attention. Then she knew. She'd use his middle name: she knew all the players' middle names.

'THEO JAMES WALCOTT! THEO JAMES WALCOTT!'

Immediately she saw Theo Walcott turn towards her with a surprised look on his face. Her trick had worked. Now that he was looking her in the eye, she had to get it right.

'THE AMBULANCE. HELP IT GET THROUGH. PLEASE.'

Theo Walcott looked round and saw the ambulance. He stuck a thumb up to Lily, then acted quickly, speaking to his teammates, pointing at Lily, who watched in amazement as the England team fanned out in their blue suits, easing the crowd backwards, gradually making a perfect path for the ambulance to come through the crowd. It was like something out of a film and it filled her with hope that Lesh might live.

With a clear path, the ambulance manoeuvred down the side of the church, its paramedics acting swiftly, finding and examining Lesh, then putting him into a moulded plastic stretcher that would support his neck and his back, in case he had injured them. They beckoned Lily to come with them.

Lily was just getting into the ambulance when she saw Kester, Hatty and Adnan standing a little way back. Hatty and Kester seemed to be holding Adnan up. It looked odd. Lily wanted to know what had happened to them. Had they managed to get the other two men? Was everything safe now? Had they found Jim?

As she stared – uncomprehending – at her friends, Lily saw Kester, Hatty and Adnan each stick up a thumb. The other two men had been dealt with: she knew that for sure. They had succeeded in stopping the attack.

Mission accomplished.

Lily tried to speak to Kester through her mic one more time, just to say well done, but it was no use. They would have to do that later. And, anyway, she had Lesh to worry about. This was no time for celebrating.

And now the ambulance was ready to leave.

Lily knew her duty was to Lesh and that the others

could look after whatever else needed dealing with, so she turned and went to sit next to her friend in the ambulance, only to find someone else was sitting in there too, concealed from the others.

Kester led Hatty and Adnan back to the hotel.

For a couple of minutes the three Squad members edged through the crowds of people without speaking. They were shattered.

Eventually Adnan spoke. 'We should be celebrating. We stopped the attack.'

Kester put his arm round his friend and smiled.

'Not until we know Lesh is OK,' Hatty said. 'Not until we find Jim. We go back to the hotel and start looking.'

BREAKING AND ENTERING

Kester, Hatty and Adnan walked out of the city centre towards their hotel. It was a twenty-minute journey among the crowds of people heading back to their homes and offices, crowds who had seen the England players, unaware that a major terror attack on their city had just been averted.

'What now?' Hatty asked.

'Try Jim again?' Kester suggested.

'No,' said Hatty. 'It's time to call Julia.'

Kester sighed. He knew she was right. They had tried Jim again and again. Julia was his commander too, so they needed to call her now. 'Is your SpyPhone working yet?' he asked the other two. Both shook their heads.

'We need a public phone booth then.'

They walked towards a cluster of apartment blocks near the Cracovia football stadium and quickly found a public phone. Kester dialled the emergency number Julia had asked them all to memorize before they headed off to Poland. He suddenly felt very tired: it had been a tough week.

The phone rang three times, then the line went quiet. Kester tried the number again. Now the line was dead.

'Nothing,' he told Hatty and Adnan.

'That's it then,' Hatty said. 'No Jim. No Julia. No SpyPhones. No nothing. What do we do?'

Kester sensed panic – or anger – in Hatty's voice. He knew this was the time for him to be strong and calm, even though he felt exactly the same as she did deep inside. He led the other two out of the housing estate and into the open parkland as they talked.

'We go back to the hotel,' Kester said, understanding what they had to do now. 'We look for Jim. If we can't find him, we break into his room and search for something to tell us what's going on.'

Jim was not at the hotel. They knocked on his door, searched every public space and corridor, but there was no sign of him. So they went looking for the other footballers.

As expected, Rio and Finn were playing *FIFA 12* in Rio's room. Neither had seen Jim either.

'He wasn't at breakfast – or here to take training,' Rio explained.

'Why don't you take a training session, Rio?' Kester suggested. 'We'll try and track down Jim.'

Rio seemed pleased at that. 'Do you think that'll be OK?'

'Yes,' Kester replied. 'Everyone looks up to you. And you're the captain.'

Rio immediately started organizing players for a training session.

With Rio and the others out of the way, Kester could do what he wanted to do next. He stood at the turn in the hotel corridor and as Adnan covered a CCTV camera with a small piece of card, Hatty walked up to Jim's room and, using her SpyPhone, decoded his door. A green light came on and Hatty was in.

Kester watched as Hatty disappeared, listening to the bangs of cupboard doors and the creak of a bed being moved before he saw Hatty emerge from the room.

'Nothing,' she said, when they were back on the fire exit staircase.

'What?' Adnan asked.

'Jim's room is empty. All his bags and clothes and everything. Gone.'

Another silence. Kester closed his eyes. Then his earpiece crackled. Their comms were back on.

'Kester?' It was Lily.

'Lily? What's going on? Is Lesh OK?'

'I'm in my room,' she said. 'You'd all best come in here.'

*

The three children filed into Lily's room. She looked grave and pale. They heard a flush coming from behind the bathroom door.

'Lesh?' Hatty said. 'Is he OK?'

Lily shook her head. 'It's not Lesh.'

'Jim?' Adnan asked.

'No,' Lily replied as the bathroom door opened and a figure appeared.

'Julia!' Kester gasped.

After they had got over their initial shock, Julia asked the children to sit down.

'We've a lot to get through,' she said as they found chairs and window ledges to perch on and Julia flicked her scrambler on.

'Lily? Update everyone on Lesh. They'll want to know.'

'Lesh is OK,' Lily explained. 'Well, he's not OK. He fell inside the cathedral tower. It looks like he's broken a leg and an arm. But they're not sure yet. He –'

'Lily saved his life,' Julia interrupted. 'She gave him mouth-to-mouth. She also stopped Svid from firing the rocket launcher. He's dead.'

'The other men have been arrested too,' Kester said, leaning across and touching Lily on the shoulder.

'Yes,' Julia said. 'I have some information from the Polish authorities, who found them inside a sculpture apparently. Who arranged that?'

'Adnan did it,' Kester said, grinning. 'He was brave.'

'It strikes me,' Julia said, 'that you've all been brave. You have achieved something amazing, this week. You stopped an attack on the England team. You made sure all three attackers were apprehended. You should all be very proud of yourselves.'

'Thank you,' Kester said. 'But what about . . .'

'What about Jim Sells?' Julia said.

'Yes.'

'He's gone.'

'Dead?'

'No, he was working with Svid. He's gone. I don't think we'll ever see him again.'

The four children said nothing. They just stared at Julia.

THE UNTHINKABLE

'WHAT?' Lily shouted.

'He's been . . . ?' Hatty couldn't finish her sentence.

'Working with Svid,' Julia confirmed.

'No.' Adnan was shaking his head. He felt sick.

The four children stared speechlessly at each other, their eyes red.

'You must have made a mistake,' Kester said. 'How can you know?'

'I know.'

'HOW?' Hatty shouted. She felt as if all the rules of how to behave with Julia had been shattered.

'Jim contacted me,' Julia said calmly. 'To ask if you were all OK.'

'This is crazy,' Lily said. 'I thought the . . .'

'. . . the world of him,' Hatty said. 'So did I.'

'He phoned me,' Julia continued. 'From some-where in Ukraine, I think.'

'Are you saying he was behind all this and he wants to know if we're OK? I . . .'

185

'He was working with Svid?' Kester whispered. 'How? Why?'

'He was working with Svid and against us. But maybe not you. If you think about it, he meant you to be miles away when all the trouble happened. That's why you ended up by Lake Roznowskie, when all the action was going on in Krakow. I understand he tried to stop the helicopter coming to get you. That's what gave me a hint that something was going on. But I think he was trying to protect you.'

'Yeah, right,' Hatty snorted. 'But he's happy for the England team to be killed?'

'Yes,' said Julia, 'it seems like he was happy for that to happen.'

'I don't understand,' Adnan said. 'He's English. He played for England.'

Lily was shaking her head. 'But why? How could anyone want that?'

Julia stepped forward and put her hand on Lily's shoulder. 'It's perhaps not that he wanted it to happen. It might be more like he couldn't stop it happening.'

'Yes, he could,' Lily spat. 'If he knew about it, he must have been part of it.'

'Lily, he's a spy,' Julia said. 'Or an agent. We don't even know who for. It's a complex world.'

'There's nothing complex about killing people!' Lily shouted. 'People with families. What's complex about that?'

'Lily's right,' Hatty said. 'It's disgusting. It's like you think this is OK, Julia.'

'No,' Julia said, her voice calm. 'If we see him, we will have to deal with him. I'm just trying to say that, as spies, we have to understand why he did what he did from his point of view.'

'We've been so stupid,' Lily growled.

'No, Lily.' Julia raised her voice for the first time. 'I'm the one who was stupid actually. I was the one who took on Jim to command this mission. I vetted him and he was as clean as a whistle. My intelligence failed. Jim is as good a sleeper agent as there could be. And as bad a traitor. What you, Lily, should be telling yourself is not that you let everyone down, but that you saved the day. You were at the sharp end of all the missions. You terminated Svid. You saved Lesh's life. You saved the England team from being blown up.'

'This is awful,' Lily said.

Now Julia was shouting. 'What was the purpose of your mission?'

The Squad reeled. Julia never shouted.

'To stop the attack on the –' Adnan started.

'To stop the attack on the England team and make sure all those involved were caught,' Julia interrupted. 'And did you achieve that?'

'Yes,' Kester answered.

'So your mission was successful. A hard mission. Made harder by your commander in the field being against you from the start. This should be a time to celebrate,' Julia said, staring at Lily. 'You have done an amazing thing for your country.'

'I don't feel like celebrating,' Lily said sullenly. She looked at Kester and Hatty and Adnan. 'Do you want to celebrate?'

All three shook their heads, frowning.

'Well,' Julia said, softening her tone, 'take it from me, you are national heroes. You might not feel like it now, but you are and one day I hope you will celebrate.'

'I might celebrate if I hear that Jim is dead,' Lily said, her voice wobbling. 'All I want now is to get out of here and go back to England.'

'That might be so,' Julia said.

'What does that mean?' Hatty asked. 'Can't we go home now?'

'There's unfinished business,' Julia smiled.

'What's that?'

'The game against Russia.'

'No way,' Hatty said. 'We're not playing that.'

TEAM PLAYERS

'WHAT'S GOING ON?'

Georgia was shouting at the back four: Kester, Hatty, Lily and Johnny, who had been slotted in to take Lesh's place. England versus Russia. The Russian players were heading for the dressing rooms, applauded by the two thousand or so fans who had come to watch the final of this international youth tournament.

It was England 0 Russia 2. Half-time.

'It's hard,' Kester said to Georgia as the other players gathered round in a circle on the pitch, 'without Lesh. We're struggling. We need more support from the midfield.'

But he knew it wasn't true. The fact was the Squad were shattered after days and nights of football and missions – and confused by everything to do with Jim and Julia and Lesh. They'd told the footballers Lesh had had a fall in the church. Nothing else.

'No, you don't need more support from the

midfield!' Georgia yelled. 'You're playing like you did against the Faroes. Really, really badly. Like you've never played football before in your lives. This is the final of a major tournament. We could have won something today. There's a trophy. We're representing our country. We've already lost and it's not even half-time . . .'

Rio put his hand on Georgia's shoulder. 'Cool it, Georgia. We're missing Lesh. He was badly injured. And Jim's gone, so we've no coach. Let's not get too upset with each other about this.'

Hatty nodded as Rio spoke. She couldn't believe how mature he was being.

'Not too upset?' Georgia shouted. 'Look over there.'

The team watched as a row of men in blue suits emerged from one of the executive boxes and listened as the fans in the stadium began to applaud them. The full men's England team. Wayne Rooney. Theo Walcott. And the rest.

'We're meeting them after the game!' Georgia shouted. 'How do you think that's going to go when we've been slaughtered? It'll be embarrassing. I can't believe this.'

Kester watched Georgia with interest, then Rio and the others. They all looked crestfallen. Kester knew this was the biggest moment of their lives, playing in this final, watched by the proper England team. And, at the same time, he was conscious that the game meant nothing to him and the Squad members. Not after everything that had gone on.

Having said her piece, Georgia stormed off the pitch towards the dressing room, followed by the rest of the footballers. Kester held back, indicating that Lily, Hatty and Adnan should too. He had something to say.

But Hatty was the first to speak. 'I hate Georgia. She's such a –'

'Yes,' Kester interrupted, 'she's annoying, but think about it.'

'Think about what?'

'This is her big moment. She's a young girl who's good at football, her heroes are about to watch her play and she's on the losing team.' Kester paused. 'And take Rio. He could get picked up by a Premier League team if one of the coaches watching sees him do well. And look at Johnny and Finn and all the others. The reason we're losing is because the four of us can't be bothered.'

'So tell them what we've been through,' Hatty said.

'We can't,' said Kester. 'You know that. We never tell people about what we do. We stick together as a small team and try to get things right for each other. Now I think we need to stick together as a larger team, as a football team. Maybe we should forget about our problems and do something for them. Julia said we should celebrate. But we know we can't, not after everything with Jim and Lesh. How about we celebrate by beating Russia at football?'

Kester looked at the other three, then at Hatty alone. He could see that Hatty was thinking about Georgia and how she hated her, but also about how they maybe owed the footballers something.

'I'm sorry to say,' Hatty muttered, 'that you're right.' She stood up. 'We need to do this for Rio, for the team. Even for Georgia.'

Something changed in the second half, a new electricity running through the team.

The key to it was Rio and Hatty. Now that Hatty was supporting Rio, Rio was supporting her. They had the centre of the pitch completely sewn up.

There was only going to be one result in the game now.

Goal one came eleven minutes into the second half. Johnny knocked a pass back to Hatty. Hatty drew a couple of defenders and laid a slide-rule pass in to Rio, who flipped the ball into space for Georgia to hit it at the Russian keeper. The keeper spilled it and there was Finn clipping in the loose ball.

1–2.

No one celebrated. Rio just grabbed the ball out of the net and put it back on the centre spot.

Goal two was all Rio's. Taking the ball from Hatty

again, he ran through six Russian tackles, and blasted the ball in off the crossbar.

2–2.

Again there were no celebrations. This time Hatty got the ball and tossed it to the referee for the restart. But she did glance up at the men's England team watching to see that they were all on their feet clapping. Hatty jogged past Georgia and pointed it out. She was surprised to see Georgia actually smile.

Having been two up and now losing the advantage, the Russian team looked more and more ragged. Bad tackle after bad tackle came in, ugly challenges that the referee had no choice but to deal with strictly. Russia lost one defender for two pushes on England players. And another who received a straight red for trying to decapitate Lily with a two-footed aerial tackle.

Russia were down to nine players: England utterly on top.

With fifteen minutes to go, Hatty ran another ball into Rio's feet, their new-found partnership cutting Russia to ribbons. But this time, rather than holding back, she ran on into the space that the missing players had left in the defence. Rio held the ball, then released it just as she was level with the defenders.

Hatty couldn't have asked for a better pass.

She steadied the ball with her first touch and was about to shoot when she saw Georgia running in beside her. Hatty hesitated, then slid the ball into the path of Georgia, who hit it hard.

The shot was unstoppable. It almost ripped the net.

3–2.

When the final whistle went, all the England players – Squad and non-Squad – ran into a huddle, their arms waving above their heads, punching the air, screaming. Kester saw Lily, Hatty and Adnan celebrating wildly, then ran to join them, jumping on their backs.

This was celebrating. If only the others knew just what they were really celebrating.

Then, as the furore died down, Kester noticed that Rio was not among them. He looked across the pitch towards the tunnel and saw their captain. He had his shirt off and was among all the Russian players, shaking their hands, then swapping his shirt with their captain.

Ten minutes later, Rio had another captain's role to perform as he led the team towards the trophy that had been put in front of the main stand on a presentation table. The crowd applauded loudly, including the full England team in the executive boxes.

Hatty watched as she saw the beaming smiles on the footballers' faces when they were presented with their winners' medals. She knew now that Kester had been right: they'd owed the footballers this.

When they all had their medals, the trophy was

handed to Rio, who lifted it high above his head. Kester, Adnan, Hatty and Lily joined the other players dancing around under a shower of ticker tape that was coming down on them, just like you'd see when the Champions' League trophy is presented.

Sitting in disguise, Julia watched from the seats. She smiled. It was good to see the four members of the Squad celebrating something, even if they were too upset to celebrate the successful service they had done for their country.

Then she glanced at her watch. The Squad were due on a flight that departed in three hours' time. She needed them back in England: a serious threat to the UK and the world was developing and she wanted them back in training as soon as possible.

But first there was the matter of the footballers meeting the England men's team.

THANK YOUS

I'd like to thank several people for helping me to write this novel. In schools I am often asked do I get help writing my books. The answer is yes.

My first reader is my wife. She reads each book through as I am writing it and then tells me where it needs a bit more work. She's got a really good eye for it and is always very very honest. Her comments allowed me to make massive changes after the first draft so, thanks to my wife, the book is a lot stronger.

My daughter helps me too. We talk through ideas for the story and she helps me name the characters. I also read parts to her to see what she thinks of them. I always listen to what she says.

Black Op is dedicated to Jim Sells: the real one. The real Jim is not a double-crossing double-agent evil spy. The real Jim Sells is a friend of mine who helps encourage millions of children to read every year through his work for the National Literacy Trust, and who also knows a lot about miltary matters. He gave me lots of good military ideas for the story, as well as telling me where I had made stupid mistakes. Jim is – in real life – a West Ham fan, but we remain friends even so. He is also a great dad to his children.

I am in a writers' group. I meet with James, Rachel and Anna in Todmorden every few weeks and we critique each other's books. It is very helpful. I still think I would not have been published if I had not been in this group, so thanks to the group's members, present and past.

Thanks too to David Luxton, my agent and friend. And Diane Baker, a teacher I work with a lot (who is also a friend).

Puffin is an amazing publisher. Dozens of people work at Puffin to make the books happen. They have lots of different roles, from editing the book to distributing it to bookshops and libraries around the world. Thank you to Puffin, especially the book's editor, Alex, who worked hard to make me work harder.

Thanks finally to the 100,000+ readers that I meet every year in schools, libraries, bookshops, festivals and online. I have asked them lots of questions about this book as I was working on it. Their answers helped me make it as good as I could.

Read more of the Squad's thrilling adventures in

THE SQUAD

WHITE FEAR

coming soon

Ten things you (possibly) didn't know about TOM PALMER

Tom was possibly left as newborn in a box at the door of an adoption home in 1967.

He has got an adopted dad and a step-dad, but has never met his real dad.

Tom's best job – before being an author – was a milkman. He delivered milk for nine years.

He once scored two goals direct from the corner flag in the same game. It was very windy.

Tom did not read a book by himself until he was seventeen.

In 1990 Tom wrecked his knee while playing for Bulmershe College in Reading. He didn't warm up and has regretted it ever since.

He was the UK's 1997 Bookseller of the Year.

He met his wife in the Sahara Desert.

Tom has been to watch over 500 Leeds United games, with Leeds winning 307. He once went for twenty-one years without missing a home game. His wife has been ten times, with Leeds winning every time.

Tom once met George Best in a London pub. Tom wanted to borrow his newspaper to find out the football scores. George kindly obliged.

It all started with a Scarecrow

Puffin is over seventy years old.
Sounds ancient, doesn't it? But Puffin has never been
so lively. We're always on the lookout for the next big
idea, which is how it began all those years ago.

Penguin Books was a big idea from the mind of
a man called Allen Lane, who in 1935 invented
the quality paperback and changed the world.
**And from great Penguins, great Puffins grew,
changing the face of children's books forever.**

The first four Puffin Picture Books were hatched in 1940 and the
first Puffin story book featured a man with broomstick arms called
Worzel Gummidge. In 1967 Kaye Webb, Puffin Editor, started the
Puffin Club, promising to **'make children into readers'**.
She kept that promise and over 200,000 children became devoted
Puffineers through their quarterly instalments of *Puffin Post*.

Many years from now, we hope you'll look back and
remember Puffin with a smile. **No matter what your age
or what you're into, there's a Puffin for everyone.**
The possibilities are endless, but one thing is for sure:
whether it's a picture book or a paperback, a sticker book
or a hardback, **if it's got that little Puffin
on it – it's bound to be good.**

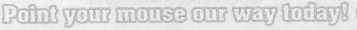